PUFI

OLLIE AND THE BOGLE

When Ollie first meets the bogle at the bottom of the garden, she half thinks it must have been a trick of her over-vivid imagination. But the bogle reappears, and gives her instructions not to let her father cut down an eldertree which is its home.

Ollie is already in trouble at school, but things go from bad to worse when the bogle puts a curse on Ollie's home and family. First a windowpane in Ollie's bedroom shatters, then the freezer defrosts itself, and then all Ollie's schoolbooks are torn to shreds. And that's just the beginning! Ollie must do as the bogle says if she wants the wizened little tree spirit to stop working against her and work for her instead.

OLLIE AND THE BOGLE

Julia Jarman

PUFFIN BOOKS

PUFFIN BOOKS

Published by the Penguin Group
27 Wrights Lane, London W8 5TZ, England
Viking Penguin Inc., 40 West 23rd Street, New York, New York 10010, USA
Penguin Books Australia Ltd, Ringwood, Victoria, Australia
Penguin Books Canada Ltd, 2801 John Street, Markham, Ontario, Canada L3R 1B4
Penguin Books (NZ) Ltd, 182–190 Wairau Road, Auckland 10, New Zealand

Penguin Books Ltd, Registered Offices: Harmondsworth, Middlesex, England

First published by Andersen Press Limited 1987
Published in Puffin Books 1989
1 3 5 7 9 10 8 6 4 2

Made and printed in Great Britain by
Cox & Wyman Ltd, Reading
Filmset in Linotron 202 Palatino

Chapter 1

Sitting at the back of the class, Ollie wondered. Had she seen it or hadn't she?

'I think you had better come and sit near the front, Olwen. You've been staring into space for the last ten minutes.'

That awful la-di-da voice!

'Come on now, swap with Melanie – and bring your books with you, child. The holidays finished yesterday.'

Ollie humped her things to the front, passing smirking Melanie Laxton on the way. Trust Melanie to have achieved Wonderful Pupil status already. Honestly, teachers were thick; they were all taken in by Melanie, had no idea what a hypocrite she was.

'Come on now, Olwen, I said the holidays were over.'

They were, worse luck; the summer holidays had ended, just when they'd started to be interesting. Ollie needed to think and it was impossible under the laser stare of Burridge. Why couldn't she be like other teachers and spend the first lesson faffing? Oh no, she was looking at her again. Better do some work. This year was going to be awful. Just look at her now, gouging red crosses on some poor victim's book.

'Olwen!' Purple-rimmed glasses glared at her.

No good, if she were going to think about her other problem she must look as if she were doing maths. She stared at her book. Whom could she tell? Who would believe her? Out of the corner of her eye she examined the class. Jason was adding fresh gum to the wad beneath his desk. David was trying to stand his pencil case on end. They'd both fall about laughing. Tracy looked as if she were painting a snowstorm with Tippex. She'd ask to see it, but what if it wasn't there? She'd only seen it once herself. Besides Tracy would blab to Melanie. No, she couldn't tell her. If only Becky hadn't left; she'd have told her. Or would she? Probably not.

The more she thought about it, the more impossible it seemed. She sometimes wondered if she believed it herself. Had it really happened or was it one of her stories? She had got a vivid imagination. Everybody said so. 'Olwen has a very vivid imagination but can't spell.' That's what her last school report had said.

'Olwen!' Burridge was beaming hate rays at her. Ollie sighed and tried to work out the area of a triangle. Who cared? What time was it? 3.55. No, she couldn't tell anyone; they'd think she was crazy, but at four o'clock she'd race home, go down to the henhouse and thoroughly investigate. If she saw it again she'd tell someone – perhaps – but not Melanie or Tracy. They'd driven her mad today with their stupid game of 'Do you want to know a secret?' Secret! Now if they'd seen what she'd seen, they'd have something to boast about – if she'd seen it, that is . . . Crikey – 3.59 – she'd better get on; bit late, oh good 4.00 already. The bell. Quick, stuff books in bag and out before the rush! Oh no, bogeyhead again.

'Class, quiet, QUIET!' She waited for silence. 'Now put your books on the right-hand corner of my desk as you leave. All except you, Olwen. I would like to see yours now. I don't think you've done very much this lesson.'

Ten minutes later Ollie grabbed her bag, left the classroom and headed for the bike sheds. Everyone else had gone, but if she got a move on she could be home by half past four. Lanthwaite was about two miles from the town. As she pedalled, a dark stain spread over the hills as a cloud drifted by. Always those hills, in whatever direction you looked, changing colour; they seemed to breathe. Like huge slumbering beasts they were . . . Stop! There she was again, imagining things. She must stop it, mustn't imagine anything. A mountain was a mountain. A tree was a tree. A face was a . . . well, she would see.

'Best place in the world, this,' her dad said. It was lovely though. Lakes and mountains. People came miles to see. That's why they had the boarding house.

Fortunately there was no one staying this week. The whole world had gone back to school, poor world, and when Ollie reached home her mother was standing in the kitchen, the kettle boiling, jam-tarts on the table.

'Just one each, dear, or maybe two, and then I'll put them away.'

It was always the same this snack as soon as she came in. But today she mustn't stop and talk, must get outside quickly.

'Just one, Mum, no really' – she was putting two on her plate – 'and no sugar please.'

Mrs Hindmarch tipped it back into the basin. 'You're not fat, Olwen, you're just nice. Now what have they given you tonight? Not a lot I hope, there's a lovely film on the telly.'

Ollie poured more milk in her tea and gulped it down. Then, eating tarts with her mother seemed a good idea, not scary like being alone at the bottom of the garden, waiting for weird . . . but no. She stood up. She must sort this matter out once and for all.

'I'll just nip and see if there are any eggs, Mum.'

'Oh, are you, dear? Oh. I thought you'd stay in and tell me about your first day back, what teachers you'd got and so on. Oh well, change your clothes first, dear. Don't get your uniform dirty straightaway. I'll get on with the dinner.'

It was good to get out of her school clothes. She could smell disinfectant and cabbage as she pulled off her grey jumper. Jeans lay tidily on the bed. Looking around she was even more convinced she'd find nothing down the garden. Her life was too ordinary. She had a nice ordinary mother, well ordinary except for being almost too nice, and a bad-tempered ordinary father.

She looked out of the window. Saw Kanathra, solid and dark, a gargantuan hump against the sky. The back garden rose steeply, was part of the mountain really. The henhouse was hidden by the toolshed. That's where she'd first seen it, at the foot of the elderberry tree. The thing. She hadn't known what to call it. It wasn't human and it wasn't any animal she could recognize. It was last Thursday, very early. They'd got up at six to go to Stockport as her aunt was ill. Ollie had gone to feed the hens and caught sight of a huge cobweb in the lower branches of the eldertree. It glistened with dew and she'd moved forward to get a closer look and then she'd seen it, the other side of the web, a spiky sort of face with dark eye sockets. No eyes that she could see, but it had stared, and she had stared, and then her father had shouted. When she went back to have another look after throwing the corn in the run, it had gone.

Common sense told her it must have been her imagination. It was a misty morning, the sort you sometimes get before a very hot day. There was a breeze and little swirly mists shook the webs which she could now see were all about her. If you stared at them long enough you could see faces in all of them, in anything – clouds, water, leaves, the pattern on the carpet even. She had imagined it, she must have.

But she hadn't. For a start, it wasn't just the staring face. It had hands too – if that was the right word – and it had pointed at her with a long spiky finger. Ollie shivered. She hadn't imagined that. She pulled on a shirt and went downstairs.

Outside it was cold and dull, a grey day. Leaves had lost their summer brightness, were waiting for autumn's colour. In the border a few marigolds blazed and a late swallow sat on the telegraph wire.

'You'll need these, dear.' Her mother had opened the kitchen door and stood there with a bowl and an anorak.

'For the eggs, Ollie. Eggs, you were going to collect them. Remember? And put on your anorak, it's cold.'

'Oh, yes, thanks.' Ollie took them.

She walked quietly across the lawn and then down the path by the vegetables, to the toolshed. Only then could she see the tree, hanging over the sheds creating a dark cave behind them. Black berries hung from red stems. The trunk was twisted and split, the leaves dull. Ollie stood for a moment and then opened the hen-house door.

There were no eggs. A brown hen sat in a nesting box clucking softly. Ollie stroked its head and then closed the door quietly, walked round the back and crouched down. It was at this level that she had seen it before. She peered into the lower branches. It was dark. Impossible to see anything. The henhut on one side, the toolshed on the other and the tree itself cut off the light. She looked at the ground. Bare earth. No bird droppings even. And it was oddly silent. No birdsong at all.

Through a gap in the branches she could see the sky. Empty. No, there was something. She squinted to see better. And high above, arched wings beat soundlessly. Swooped, beat again. The peregrine falcon in lonely wander. She couldn't be sure, but it would account for the silence of the other birds. Ollie recalled the spring, happy times, weekends on Ghyll Crag with her father, watching the parent falcons, guarding the eggs. And then the disappointment weeks later, when they learned the eggs had been stolen, replaced by hens' eggs. Nobody knew when or how. Was that when things had started to go wrong? Was that why her father was so bad-tempered these days?

Ollie listened and waited and hoped no one would come down the garden. She would feel very stupid sitting on her heels staring at a tree. She could say she was bird-watching. She looked up. One problem – no birds. The falcon had gone. There wasn't a chaffinch or sparrow in the tree. Not a rook or a crow in the sky. It was very odd. You could almost hear the silence tingling.

She found a piece of stick and poked about the soil, uncovered a few worms and put them in the egg bowl. Perhaps her dad could use them as fishing bait. A beetle scurried over a piece of wood. She turned the wood over and watched a coppery centipede race for the cover of a paint can. No, she must have been mistaken. This was a perfectly ordinary bottom of a garden, like anybody else's, a place where you dumped things which you meant to get rid of but hadn't got round to yet. There was an old wheelbarrow, several rusty bike frames, a pile of black and white tiles and a couple of old lavatories which they had taken out of the house when they were smartening it up for visitors. Definitely not the setting for . . . well . . . things.

Ollie started to think about her day at school. Why had Tracy and Melanie suddenly gone off her? They'd called round yesterday and said they were starting packed lunches – and then gone into school dinners. She'd had to eat her sandwiches on her own – well, not completely, there was Hazel the new girl who'd lived in America . . .

Ou–ch! Pins and needles in her right foot! She must scratch it. No good. She stood up and stamped on the ground. It still prickled. She stamped again, harder. No, no, it was driving her crazy. She would have to take her boot off. So, leaning on the henhouse she pulled off her wellington and gripped her foot hard. That helped. The tingling began to ease off.

And then it happened – the sharp sting on her right cheek. As she looked up her hand shot to her face – and there it was. The same face beneath the leaves, peering over the edge of the guttering, pointing at her with a spiky claw. She stood there on one leg unable to move, unable to stop staring at its eyes which glinted from the depths of cavernous sockets – and then it vanished. There was a rustle of leaves and it vanished. She could feel it watching her, but couldn't see it. She looked down at her hand, by her side now, fingers smeared with purple juice.

Boots on, she went and looked over the fence because it could have been the boys next door. They sometimes ambushed her if they hadn't anything better to do. But the boys weren't there. She knew they wouldn't be. She knew what had thrown the elderberry. Seconds – and then it had gone, but it was enough. She couldn't mistake its long nose, glinting eyes, its accusing finger.

Most of all though, she couldn't forget the message – in elderberry juice on the grey guttering. STOP HIM it said. STOP HIM. She looked up. She couldn't forget it, because it was still there. STOP HIM, it said in wobbly capitals. What did it mean?

Chapter 2

What did it mean, 'Stop him'? Who? What? Ollie could think only of the creature in the tree. She had come in, laid the table because her mother had asked her to, washed her hands, sat down to eat, but it was as if she were in a dream. Her body was doing things in the kitchen but really she was still down the garden.

'What's up with you? Cat got your tongue?'

Ollie looked up.

'Ollie love, your dad's been talking to you for the last five minutes. It's rude, love, not to answer.'

'Oh, don't mind me, I'm just the one who earns our daily bread, that's all. Not worth interrupting madam's wonderful thoughts for.'

He carried on eating. Ollie couldn't think of anything to say.

Her mum said, 'Oh Albert love, don't say that, we all appreciate what you do, don't we, Ollie?'and then the three of them carried on eating, the chink and scrape of knives and forks the only sound.

'I'm having that tree up tonight.' Ollie was lifting a forkful of shepherd's pie to her mouth when her father spoke. 'Blasted nuisance, elder. Takes useful space and gives nowt in return.'

Tree. Did he say elder?

'If we're to have a house and garden this size every inch must earn its keep. I'll cut it down and put a compost heap there. Start tonight.'

'No, you can't.' It was as if someone else had spoken. Ollie felt herself go red.

'Oh' – Albert Hindmarch's Adam's apple bulged – 'and what's wrong with you? Who asked for your opinion? Eh, who? I'm waiting for an answer.'

'No one, but . . . but I don't think it's a good idea.' Could this be what the thing meant? Her father's neck was blotchy and his Adam's apple was jumping up and down. She ought to keep quiet. 'You're not supposed to cut down trees, there's a shortage and . . . and the birds eat the berries and insects lay eggs on them . . . and . . . other birds . . .' Her voice tailed off. He should know that anyway.

'Oh my, oh my, we are a mine of information, aren't we? Must write to the BBC about you, eh Mother? They might want to use our Olwen when David Attenborough's on holiday, or that other naturalist fellow, the one with the beard. Be very useful to them to have someone like our Olwen standing by to spout a load of old rubbish.'

Mrs Hindmarch was making herself busy at the stove pretending not to hear. Too much to expect her to stick up for her but at least she wasn't joining in. He was talking again.

'And let me tell you another thing, young lady, I don't want a lot of creepy-crawlies creepy-crawling all over my garden, eating all my fruit and vegetables. And shall I tell you why?' He didn't wait for an answer. 'Because that garden is part of our bread and butter. It's what we feed our visitors on. It's what we feed ourselves on. It's what keeps you in disco outfits and fancy hair stuff.'

So that's what it was. The one new outfit her mum had bought her out of the summer profits. Mean old so-and-so.

'Come on now, Albert, finish up, dear, while it's still warm. I've got some nice baked apples for afters.'

There was her mum again soothing, calming. Still there was no point in riling him. She had to stop him cutting down the tree.

'Apple, Olwen?'

'No thank you.' Her mum's niceness irritated her as much as her dad's temper these days.

'Don't speak to your mother like that, Olwen.'

'Oh, it's all right, dear, she said "thank you", didn't you, love?'

'Yes, sorry Mum, but I'm full.'

Her mum brought her father his pudding. Ollie sat waiting. What could she do? She looked down at her bitten nails. How could she stop him destroying the eldertree? What could she say to him? It wasn't beautiful. Birds didn't eat the berries – she'd noticed that today. It was as if they avoided it. And she'd often heard people say elder was a nuisance – like ivy – it grew anywhere and choked other things. If he'd said a fortnight ago he was cutting it down she wouldn't have noticed. But now, because of a message from a small spiked creature, in elderberry juice, on a piece of guttering . . . No! She shook her head. No! Definitely not. It was crazy. Bonkers. Impossible. She was risking life and limb – well, pocket money and Friday night youth club – to save a rotten old tree that she'd hardly noticed before last week . . . no, it was crazy. Hell's bells – he'd finished eating! Impossible. So why did she feel compelled to stop him? Why? Crikey, he was scraping his chair back now.

'Thanks, Mother, that was very nice, not too starchy and I'll go and work off what starch there was, cutting down that tree. Hey, Olwen? Are you coming out to give your dad a hand?' Cheerful now! But still giving orders. What could she *do*? She had to stop him. Had to.

'Er . . .' She rushed over to the kettle. 'Would you like a cup of coffee, Dad, or tea?'

'No, no. Thanks, love. Later. Best get on. It's dark by eight.'

He was at the back door. What now? She dashed after him. 'Dad, you ought to change. You've still got your work clothes on.'

'No, no, these'll do. Stop bossing, can't stand bossy women.'

He opened the door. Strode down the garden. She ran to catch up.

'Dad.'

He didn't hear her.

'Dad, I don't think you should.'

He was whistling now.

'What's that, Olwen? Hold on while I get my saw.'

He was inside the toolshed. Idea! Crazy. She knew it was, but couldn't stop herself. Bang! The door slammed shut. Key now. Where? No key! No keyhole even. Mad! Why hadn't she checked?

'O . . . llieeee!! – what the hell are you doing? Open that door!'

She just stood there, expecting him to break through, steam puffing from his nostrils like a cartoon character. But first the door opened, crashing against the side of the shed. Then he appeared, red and angry.

'What the h . . .'

'S-sorry, Dad. W-wind I think.'

He stood there, breathing heavily, then spat on the ground. Gave her a look as if she'd just squirmed out of it.

'Wind,' he spat again, looked up. 'Stupid, that's what you are.'

There wasn't so much as a breeze.

'I'll sort you out later.'

He stormed round the back of the shed, head down and shoulders raised. Ollie followed, watched as he stood and sized up the tree, planned his attack.

She felt stupid and frightened, looked up to the roof of the shed. Saw a pink smear where the writing had been. She stared at the tree. Nothing. Ash trees bordering the hen run stirred. A cluck came from the hen-house where the hens had already gone to roost, but there was nothing else. No face, no pointing finger.

'Best get moving.' Ollie jumped. He began to chop at some of the smaller branches near the bottom and she felt sick; her throat hurt as if her tonsils were blocking it. She swallowed hard trying to bring saliva to her mouth.

'Blasted tree!' He was wiping the sweat from his forehead, a few ragged branches at his feet. He raised the axe again, hacked away higher up.

'Damn tree. Dead wood most of this, should come away easily.'

Deadwood. Dreadwood. Perhaps she needn't do anything after all. Perhaps the tree could protect itself. It didn't seem to want to be cut down. She looked at her father. He'd put down the axe, and was rolling up his sleeves. Sweat made his bald head shine. Oh, now he was picking up the big bow saw. He was angry. She saw him step forward then lunge at the tree.

For several minutes his arm moved backwards and forwards, backwards and forwards, veins bulging, saw screaming and screeching. Icy shivers ran through Ollie but she couldn't move away. Hands tight over her ears, she watched, fascinated, as he pushed and pulled with all his strength and the tree just stood there resisting the steel teeth tearing into its centre. She heard her father grunting and snorting, saw him getting angrier. Then she saw the tree shudder, heard it groan, saw it stagger from side to side, watched it . . . falling towards her . . .

'Move!'

'Move!'

'Silly little *fool*!'

The tree was at her feet, and her father's hand was gripping her arm. He was glaring at her. They were standing on the path by the chicken house door.

'Silly little fool!'

Ollie pulled away from him. Her arm hurt and she felt dizzy, didn't know what had happened.

'I told you to move. Told you it was falling.' Sweat trickled down his face. 'Thank God I was fast enough to grab you.'

There was no point in speaking. She looked down at the felled tree, saw bleeding berries at her feet, and then she looked at the piece still standing – a huge jagged splinter pointing to the sky. She looked at the branches around its base, saw the leaves stir, looked for the remnants of a spider's web, looked for . . . A distant rumbling made her look up. The sky, grey and blue, was like a stormy sea. A wind had got up and the ash trees were swaying from side to side. A leaf landed at her feet.

'Get inside. Get, I said. And straight to bed. Reckon I'll leave it for tonight.' Mr Hindmarch was picking up his tools. 'If rain holds off I'll dig the rest up tomorrow, put poison on what's left.' Ollie nodded. There was no point in arguing, but she felt hollow inside somehow, like the trunk of the eldertree, decayed, nasty . . . bad. She ought to have stopped him, ought to stop him now. The tree could still grow again, they were very hard to kill . . .

'Move, I said.'

She followed him in.

'Bed!' He jerked his head towards the hall door. Her mother was at the sink.

'Oh good, dears. Just in time. I've put the kettle on and I've put a hot-water bottle in your bed, Olwen. Summer's over I think, don't you, Albert? There's a nip in the air. Now, Olwen, if you'd like to wash and get ready I'll bring you a nice cup of tea to drink in bed . . . Is anything the matter, dears?'

It wasn't eight yet but Ollie didn't want to stay downstairs. She wanted to be on her own, wanted to think. Besides, any moment now he'd start telling her mum how stupid she was, how she'd nearly got herself killed, how he'd saved her, how she was just like her mother and hadn't got a grain of the Hindmarch common sense. And if he really went on her mother would start to cry.

She climbed the stairs slowly, undressed and got into bed.

'Here's your tea, dear.' It was her mother. She never knocked.

'I'll put it by your bed, dear. That's right, love, you get a good night's sleep, you look a bit peaky.'

Sleep? Fat chance of that. Her mind was a whirlpool.

'Olwen. Ollie love, what do you say?'

'Oh, thank you, Mum. 'Night.'

She would wash in the morning. Her feet reached for the bottle at the bottom of the bed. She drew it up and clung to it. Tried to slow down her whirling thoughts. She closed her eyes, then opened them and picked up her tea.

Well. Did this thing exist? She believed it when she saw it, but seconds afterwards she began to doubt, and after a day or two, she felt sure it was her imagination.

She had seen it – or imagined it – twice now. On both occasions it had been a Thursday. The first time was exactly a week ago, early in the morning, the second today at around five o'clock, but already it seemed a long time ago. Already her mind was filled with doubts. What did she know, think she knew, about it?

She put down her tea, got out of bed and found a pen and an old exercise book, got into bed again. She would write down everything she knew about it. It. It would be a sort of test – had she got any facts to go on? If she had she must write them down and next time she saw it, if she saw it, she would check the facts against her list, and if they were the same, well, that would prove . . . what? Well, that she wasn't making it up as she went along.

She turned to a page near the middle and wrote, underlined heavily:

THING

COLOUR – brownish with green tinges – rather like elderbery branches – camooflarg?
HABITAT – in or near elderbery tree at botom of our garden.
HIGHT – not sure. Haven't seen all of it.
SHAPE – spikey, thin, pointed nose and fingers.
OTHER BITS – deep eye sockits, posibly deep set glinting eyes.
ACTIONS – stares, throws things – elderberies to be presise, writes but doesn't say anything.
WHEN SEEN – 1) Thursday 2nd Sept. 6 a.m. approx.
WHEN SEEN – 2) Thursday 9th Sept. 5 p.m. approx.

Voices floated upstairs, her father's mainly. 'Stupid child. Lives in cloud-cuckoo-land.' Louder now, he must be coming upstairs. 'Should have seen her. Just stood there . . .' Ollie put out the light and shoved the book under her pillow. Hoped he wasn't coming to 'sort her out'. She heard the bathroom door go. Good. She'd had an idea. She wasn't stupid. There were books about such things. She'd read one once. Some people used to believe in them. What day was it tomorrow? Friday. Her year wasn't allowed in the library during dinner hour but she had a library lesson in the afternoon. If she raced through that boring session of putting stupid lists into alphabetical order she would be allowed to pick a book from the shelves. Folklore, that's what she needed – or Supernatural, even better. Lots of people were interested in that. Melanie and Tracy were always getting books out about ghosts or witches or haunted houses. Odd really, she didn't like books like that herself . . . too scary, especially at bedtime.

Next door the loo was flushed and the door opened. Footsteps went by her room and then downstairs. Good. When she heard the kitchen door close, Ollie turned on the light. Yes, it was scary. But it was scarier still not knowing. Tomorrow she would find out everything she could.

Chapter 3

Ollie didn't have to wait till the afternoon. She managed to slip into the library at dinnertime. It solved the problem of what to do with herself. Tracy and Melanie had a secret – 'Nobody else allowed'. Hazel, the new girl, had violin practice.

She found the book she wanted, but couldn't get it out. It said INFORMATION ONLY on the cover. The writing was very small and was in two columns like a bible. There was about half a page on Elderberry – *genus* Sambucus, it called it, definitely the same plant, white flowers in summer, purplish-black berries in autumn, green serrated leaves.

The first paragraph was a long list of its evil associations. The cross on which Jesus died was made of elder. Judas Iscariot hanged himself on an eldertree. The wood stank, it said, though Ollie was sure it didn't. She read on . . . 'elder only grows on ground which has been soaked in blood . . . elderwood never used in shipbuilding or in fires . . . elder cradle would cause a child to pine away . . . elder branch brought into the house in Germany brings ghosts . . . in England the devil . . .' Ollie closed the book.

Deadwood. Dreadwood. The devil. She had to force herself to read on but was glad she did. Elder could cure almost anything. Bark, berry and flower dissolved warts and warded off rheumatism; it was also good for deafness, faintness, strangulation, sore throat, ravings, snake and dog bites, insomnia, melancholy and hypochondria – and the leaves kept out flies. A force for good indeed. But it was when she turned the page she came to the really interesting bit. 'See ELDER BOGLE', it said. She scanned the page and found it right at the bottom:

'ELDER BOGLE – the spirit of the eldertree in . . .'

And then the blasted bell rang for the end of dinner hour. Three whole lessons before she could get back. She couldn't possibly stop now . . . she found the place again. 'ELDER BOGLE, spirit of the eldertree . . . *Hyldeboegl* . . .'

'Olwen Hindmarch, return the book to the shelf, and yourself to the classroom, immediately.' Miss Quinn was standing over her. 'What are you doing anyway, it's not your day? Hurry up or you'll be in trouble. Quick, I'll put it back for you, just this once. Hurry.'

Ollie hardly noticed getting downstairs, didn't see that the corridors were empty. Elder bogle? Could it be? She was late of course and Burridge summoned her.

'Well, Olwen? I'm waiting.'

Ollie tried to look abject, tried to think of something to say, but could only think of what she had read.

'I'm waiting, Olwen. Why are you late?'

'Olwen!'

'Oh. I'm sorry, Miss Burridge, but I was in the library at the top of the building and I didn't hear the bell.'

Easy. Why didn't she think of it before? Burridge was actually smiling, a repulsive sight. Teeth like cheese.

'All right then. We won't take a house point this time.' Oh goody goody. A hundred times thank you. Bow down. Lick boots. Now when could she get back to the library?

'Well, Olwen, what do you say?'

'Oh . . . er . . . thank you, Miss Burridge.'

'Very well, but don't let it happen again. Now return to your seat and,' she raised her voice, 'everyone get out your books.' Oh no, not maths. Worse, double maths, then break, then music, then library last. Two whole hours to go.

Several times during the afternoon she stared at her watch, convinced it went into reverse when she wasn't looking. She tried to get upstairs during break but a prefect blocked the way. There was a staff meeting and it was outdoor break for everyone. Melanie and Tracy had seen her heading for the library and when she did reach the yard cries of boffin and swot greeted her. They kept it up through most of break. It was a long break too. The good thing was that music was shorter, but it seemed hours later that she was climbing the stairs to the library.

She looked for a place on her own and raced through the index work, ignored the hisses of swot and boffin, and went to get the book from the shelf. She passed the window. There was no sign of rain. Tonight, if she didn't stop him, her father would destroy the tree. She carried the book to her table, found the relevant page.

'ELDER BOGLE, the spirit of the eldertree; the ancient *hyldeboegl*. Neither man nor woman would break off a sprig of elder (whether for brew or other purpose) without first invoking or apologizing to the spirit of the tree. No child would injure the branches in any way.'

Ollie copied it all down. Perhaps it had been at the bottom of the garden for centuries. Must have been there long before the house was built. She suddenly sat up straight. Here she was treating the thing as real. All her doubts seemed to have gone and it was stupid. The book was about what people believed thousands of years ago – or was it? She read it again. 'No woman would break off . . . No child would injure . . .' That 'would' could refer to past or present.

She turned to the bit she had read during the dinner hour. 'In Bohemia men tip their hats to the elder . . . in some Christian countries the tree has evil associations . . .' That was in the present tense right enough.

It was confusing. She turned back to elder bogle, wished there was a picture but it wasn't that sort of book. What did 'invoke' mean? She needed a dictionary. There was a big one on the teacher's desk. She knew what apologize meant. She was doing it all the time, but would an apology be enough? Ancient man did it if he broke off a sprig or injured a branch. Her father was cutting the whole thing down and was going to poison the root. She went to the desk to look up 'invoke'.

'Invoke, *v.t.* Call on (deity etc.) in prayer or as witness; appeal to (person's authority etc.); summon (spirit) by charms; ask earnestly for (vengeance, help, etc.).'

Summon spirit by charms would fit best, but what charms? Ask earnestly for – for what? Forgiveness? Yes she could apologize and ask for forgiveness for destroying its home. Say she was very sorry but her father had insisted and . . . and . . . there were lots of other eldertrees around. There were – thousands of them. They were in no danger of dying out or anything like that, not like elm trees. But how could she summon it? Perhaps she didn't need to. She had seen it twice, hadn't she, once without wanting to. Maybe it would appear again and this time she would talk to it. It. Bogle? Elder bogle?

The bell must have gone. The class was streaming out. Oh, here were Melanie and Tracy. She put her hands over her notes. Mr Sparrow told them to go downstairs and they scuttled off arm in arm.

'Come on now, Olwen, I've got basketball practice after school. You'll have to finish what you're doing next week.'

She took a last look at the book. Invoke, apologize. Yes, that's what she'd do. Down to the bicycle sheds now and then home. She glanced out of the window. The school bus was already leaving. Somebody was waving at her. Hazel, the new girl, she thought. Red hair anyway. Ollie waved back.

She escaped from her mother as soon as she could and went down to the bottom of the garden, not sure what she was going to do, or what would happen when she did it. The part of her that didn't believe was very scornful of the part that did. She had a good look round first. It wouldn't do to have Russell and Brett watching her. She couldn't see them but the sounds of thudding hooves and gunfire suggested they were stuck in front of their video. Everyone except the Hindmarchs had one, were always talking about the films they had seen. Horror films mainly. Funny how they loved watching that sort of thing, but if you said you'd actually seen something which wasn't quite – well – normal, you'd be the laughing-stock of the neighbourhood.

The severed trunk was still there, of course, jagged and splintery. The sawn-off bit lay on the ground, leaves limp and squashed elderberries staining the earth. She thought of blood. Life blood. Ollie bears a berry as red as any blood. She shuddered and knelt down. Took another look round to check that no one was watching, then closed her eyes and whispered. She had made up the rhyme on the way home.

'Elder bogle, elder bogle,
El El El,
Truly I'm sorry for I mean you well.'

She felt incredibly stupid, would have died if anyone had seen her. Still. Opening her eyes she looked all around. Waited. Nothing at all. But did she have to see it? It could be listening, couldn't it, hidden somewhere? She whispered again.

'Elder bogle, elder bogle,
El El El,
Truly I . . .'

She waited, kept as quiet as she could. Funny how there was no such thing as silence. You could always hear something. Close to there was the rustling sound of leaves, the scratching and clucking of hens, a twig snapping for no perceptible reason; in the distance the hum of traffic along the motorway.

She listened and watched. A shot rang out from next door, a burst of the *Play School* theme music from her own house, and then a door closing. Silly how her mum still watched that programme. Quietness again. And that odd tingling in the air that she had noticed yesterday, but not the tingling in her foot, thank heavens. There was a strange yellow light in the sky too. Something ought to happen. Her eyes travelled along the guttering, penetrated the remaining branches of the eldertree stump, but the strange spiky face wasn't there.

Evil, the book had said it was – but good too. It depended. Whatever happened, she must make sure none of the wood was brought inside. What had the book said? Elderwood brought into the house brings . . . ghosts . . . the devil? It was too horrible to think about, but she couldn't stop herself. It wasn't just the book. She'd had this feeling before she'd read it.

She waited. Looked around. In the strange yellow sky a crow cawed. If only she could see it now. If she could explain, apologize, ask what she could do to make amends. But could it tell her? It could write. Could it speak? She listened. Wanted to hear a scuffling in the leaves, to follow the sound till she saw it peering at her. At the same time she knew that when she did, she'd be afraid. Dreadwood. Deadwood. She looked at her watch. Twenty minutes she had waited. She'd try once more.

'Elder bogle, elder bogle,
El El El,
. . .

NO! NO! NO!'

She threw her head from side to side. Hated herself. Sick with disgust. What a fool she was. Her dad was right. These were crazy thoughts. She must shake them from her brain, put them back in books where they belonged. What she had been thinking was nonsense; imagination, that was all, her stupid imagination.

But gone now. Quite gone. She opened her eyes and breathed deeply. Felt calmer. There was no such thing as a tree spirit. No such thing as an elder spirit. No elder bogle. No 'thing'. Nothing at all. She glared at the tree stump. Ugly. Her father could do what he liked with it. It was nothing to do with her. It must be teatime. She turned her back on the tree, looked straight in front of her and strode down the garden path.

And, as she passed, two claws clung to the rim of the old white lavatory bowl, two glinting eyes peered over the edge, and watched her till she entered the kitchen door.

Chapter 4

After tea Mr Hindmarch said he was going to carry on cutting down the tree. A can of sodium chlorate stood by the back door, bought on his way home from work. He said it would finish off the roots. Ollie said nothing, refused even to think about it. It was none of her business. She said she would do the washing up and then get on with her homework. He went out whistling.

While Ollie washed, her mum wiped. Mrs Hindmarch talked non-stop about nothing in particular and Ollie tried hard to listen. She'd decided she would never again let her imagination get the better of her. She would concentrate on ordinary everyday things, do exactly what she was told and keep out of trouble. No more daydreaming. No more flights of fancy. Facts, she would stick to them. When she had finished she went upstairs, got her notebook out of her school bag, ripped out the pages about 'Thing' and tore them into tiny pieces. That was the end of it.

It was maths homework. Good. For the first time ever she felt satisfaction filling the squared pages with row after row of numbers. She did two problems more than necessary, a first step towards getting into Burridge's good books. Social studies next. She usually enjoyed this. Not today. 'Imagine you are a medieval peasant whose family is starving. You approach the lord of the manor to ask for more food. Write down what you will say to him.' How stupid. Here she was, trying to keep a grip on reality, being asked to write a thing like that. She closed the book. She had all weekend to do it in and she certainly didn't feel like doing it now. She would join her mother downstairs.

Mrs Hindmarch was watching *Woofety Woof*, the new television quiz programme.

'Oh, Olwen, I'm glad you've come, love. If this lass gets this one right she'll win a centrally heated dog kennel. Listen now, the questions are ever so difficult, but my, she's a clever lass, a bit like you. You know you ought to get on one of these programmes. There's lovely prizes and this Gordon Blessit, he's a scream. Listen, he's starting.'

Gordon Blessit looked as if the future of mankind depended on the answer. One hand on the arm of blonde Maureen, from West Bromwich, the other loosening his pink shirt collar, his voice shook.

'Tell me, Maureen, if you can, for a really beautiful' (he said 'bewdiful') 'centrally heated dog kennel with bone-scented blankets, and, let's not forget, a year's supply of Catso, the dog-food dogs really love, and remember, I'm so sorry, but I cannot help you on this one, so think before you answer. Timewise you have just thirty seconds to tell me, wait for it . . .' There was a loud drum roll. Maureen chewed her knuckles. Another drum roll. '. . . What was the name and breed of the dog which came last, I said last, in Scuff's Dog Show 1958?'

The studio clock ticked loudly. Gordon Blessit wrung his hands. Maureen closed her eyes, her thin face scrunched up with the effort of remembering. Ollie looked at her mother who also had her eyes closed. Incredible. And then the screen went blank. The light went out. They would never know who came last at

Scuff's in 1958, never know whether Maureen's pampered pet got a new kennel. A power cut had brought an end to their anguish. Mrs Hindmarch was upset.

'Oh Ollie love, go and get your dad.'

It was nearly dark outside. Ollie didn't want to go but she reminded herself that she was being realistic and matter-of-fact and obedient and ran to the bottom of the garden. There was nothing to be afraid of. Only babies were scared of the dark. Her father was just putting his saw away.

'Good, it's you, Olwen. I need some help. Fill that barrow with those logs will you, and wheel them down to the garage. Stack them at the side by the wall.' Logs. Elder logs. Brought into the house bring . . . No. As she picked them up she told her dad what she'd come for.

'Power cut, eh? Seems odd. Nobody else affected.'

She looked at the other houses along the ridge. He was right. All of them were brightly lit. Only theirs stood in darkness.

'More likely a fuse. I'll come in a minute. Must get these logs inside. There's going to be rain I think. In fact I think I'll do them myself. I was going to treat that stump, what's left of it, with sodium chlorate, but there's no point if it's going to rain. I'll do it tomorrow. You go along in and tell Mother I'll be along soon.'

Ollie went thankfully; it was cold outside. Besides, if she wasn't going to think about the eldertree, it was better not to see it either and that was difficult. A block and tackle was attached to the shed. Her dad had obviously tried to pull the stump out of the ground – without success. He'd then tried digging round it and chopping off the roots. Wood chips lay everywhere. As she walked back to the house she supposed even that was stupid, trying to avoid it, that is. It was just a tree, an ordinary old tree. The more she treated it like that the better. In the morning she would offer to help tidy up, burn the thin branches and so on, sweep up the leaves.

Mrs Hindmarch was sitting in front of the blank television. She had got up to make a cup of tea, then realized the kettle wouldn't work either, then hurt her knee on the corner of the fridge as she'd made her way back to her chair.

'We've got candles in the cupboard under the stairs, Olwen. You'd better get them, we don't know how long this power cut will last.'

'It isn't a power cut, Dad says. Nobody else is cut off anyhow.'

Mr Hindmarch came in about ten minutes later. He had a large torch with him, and went straight to the fuse box in the hall. When he came back to the kitchen, he was shaking his head and the lights were still out.

'Odd that, nowt wrong there.'

It was odd. The whole evening was odd, the three of them sitting round the empty fireplace, a candle in a sauce bottle on the mantelpiece. It was cold too and Mr Hindmarch's attempts to cheer them up by telling them of the hardships of his youth received only polite 'yes dears' even from Mrs Hindmarch. Ollie soon said she would go to bed.

Although only nine o'clock it was utterly dark. Her dad lent her his torch but came up for it ten minutes later. She curled up in bed trying to get warm. She'd kept her socks on because there was no hot-water bottle but her feet were still freezing. It was very quiet at the top of the house, quieter than usual, she thought. Only the occasional creak or gurgle. She lay there stiffly listening, wishing she could read, trying not to think. The wind outside had dropped and after she had lain there for some time she heard a tapping on the window. Rain, the expected rain. Must be. Quite a heavy fall, its rhythmic pattering grew louder and eventually sent Ollie to sleep.

When she woke she was surprised it wasn't morning. Why was she sitting up? Why was it still dark? In fact it wasn't quite so dark as it had been. Moonlight shone through the window. Shadows jumped on the walls. Scary. No! It was the rain which must have woken her, she decided. The tapping on the window was much louder now, more insistent, in fact not like rain at all. It must be a branch, a branch of some climbing plant which had broken away from the wall. Ivy. The wind and rain must be dashing it against the glass. That's what it was. She lay down and put her head beneath the covers to try and shut out the noise.

But if anything it got louder. It had an insistent rhythm. Tappety TAP. Tappety TAP. Tappety TAP. TAP TAP TAP!

She sat up. Help. She could see jerky movements in the gap where the curtains didn't fit properly! Her heart thumped. Stupid. There was only one thing to do. Same as when she thought there was someone under the bed or in the wardrobe. Investigate. Prove to herself there was nothing there. First, switch on the light. She felt for the switch, pressed it. Nothing happened. Remembered. Damn, the power must still be off.

TAP TAP TAP!

It was waving now – frantically. No! She must stop imagining things. It was ivy. Ivy. Go away! I'm not going to look any more! Won't listen. She closed her eyes and slid under the bedclothes, pulled the pillow over her ears and burrowed to the bottom of the bed.

Fainter and fainter the pattering grew. Ollie heard it

though clenching her ears against the sound. Fainter and fainter – until at last it stopped – and she fell asleep.

When she woke the bedroom light was on. She could hear voices below and smell toast. Pulling on her dressing-gown she went downstairs. Her mum and dad were in the kitchen drinking tea.

'Funny that. I'd better check the fuse box all the same. Might be summat loose.'

The electricity had come back on during the night, it seemed. Mr Hindmarch went off to investigate.

'Cup of tea, Olwen?'

'Yes, please.'

Saturday. It was lovely not to have to rush off to school. Her mum gave her a plate of toast and marmalade. The kitchen was warm too, not like her bedroom, and Ollie would like to have stayed there. She picked up a magazine.

'Oh come on, Ollie love, eat up and get dressed, you know your dad doesn't like you sitting around in your dressing-gown. You're lucky he hasn't said something already.'

'Yes, you are.' Her father came in frowning. 'Can't understand it. Nothing wrong there. I reckon I'll give Electricity Board a ring.'

He went into the hall and soon his angry voice was demanding to speak to someone who knew a thing or two. He was soon back. 'Some woman, said she was the manager, likely story, said there were no power cuts last night. Said nobody else had complained and had we had our wiring checked. Darned cheek. I spent a fortune on rewiring less than twelve months ago.' He caught sight of Ollie. 'You still here? Well hop it. Can't stand the sight of women in their dressing-gowns at ten o'clock in the morning. Lazy, I call it.'

Ollie hopped, or rather walked, out of the kitchen

and up the stairs huddled in her dressing-gown. She hadn't looked out of the window yet but it felt cold, wintry. It wasn't till she had hurriedly washed and dressed that she pulled back the curtains and saw it. At first she thought it was frost on the window, thick frost, but only for a few seconds. There were nine panes in all and only the centre one was cracked, shattered – in the pattern of a spider's web.

She closed the curtains and walked over to the bed, and for five minutes she just sat there shaking, her head in her hands. And then she stood up, picked up her pyjamas and put them under her pillow, straightened the bedclothes, and went downstairs closing the door behind her.

'Do you want any shopping done, Mum, I thought I would go into Helmswick on my bike?'

It was cold pedalling along and it was good to reach the town, feel the warm air blowing from the doorways of the supermarkets. It didn't take long to do her mother's shopping. She spent a quarter of an hour looking at the animals in the pet shop and then made her way to the library. She wished she could have a pet. A dog or a cat was out of the question, her father hated both, but a hamster or a guinea pig would be nice. The library was warm too. Ollie chose her books, one on cookery, one on guinea pigs, no stupid fairy stories, and then sat down to read them. She ought to be home by dinnertime, didn't want to be earlier. Sooner or later her mother or father would discover the smashed windowpane.

She supposed she should have told them herself. If it would have helped she would have, but given the choice between trouble now or trouble later, Ollie preferred it later. One thing was certain, there would be trouble. She didn't deserve it. It wasn't her fault but who would believe her? Not her father for sure.

She had thought of at least three explanations, not counting the ivy against the glass. It could have been low-flying aircraft breaking the sound barrier – there was an RAF base nearby and jet planes often screamed overhead. It could have been hailstones – it was more than rain she had heard last night. Or it could have been the boys next door. Just like Russell and Brett to throw slate chips from the drive at her window, to scare her. She couldn't see them doing it in the middle of the night though, and tried to remember when she had last seen the glass in one piece. It had been dark when she went to bed, and she supposed the curtains had been drawn earlier by her mother.

When she entered the kitchen all was quiet. Mrs Hindmarch was cooking lunch.

'It's just about ready, dear, you can tell your dad if you want. He's somewhere about fixing polythene to the windows, an idea he got from one of his Do-It-Yourself books, says it will save us hundreds of pounds on heating bills.'

He was in the top bathroom, stroking his chin and looking very pleased with himself. A large roll of polythene lay in the bath and a piece of it hung from the top of the window.

'Your room next, Olwen. I'll do it when I've finished this.'

He followed her downstairs. 'Might even fix a radiator in there for you. I got one in sale last week. Bargain it was.'

Ollie felt ill.

The eruption came about half-way through the afternoon as she was measuring out the ingredients for flapjacks. She had just stuck a spoon in the tin of golden syrup when there was a bellow, then a sound like an avalanche as her father stormed down the first flight of stairs, then another bellow as he summoned Ollie to her room.

'What have you done now, Ollie love? You'd better go. I'll look after these for you till you come down.'

But Ollie didn't come down. Mrs Hindmarch made the flapjacks herself.

Chapter 5

Prison! It was just like prison! In vain Ollie pleaded her innocence. I didn't do it. I didn't do it. She said it over and over again, but Mr Hindmarch was judge and jury and he pronounced her guilty. She stayed in her room for the rest of Saturday and all day Sunday. She would stay there, he said, till she told the truth about the window. Why had she done it? What had she done it with? Ollie wondered if he would keep her off school, but on Monday morning her mum told her to get ready. She was to go to school but must return to her bedroom as soon as she got home. She was to eat her meals in her room – and no puddings. Her father didn't want to speak to her till she was prepared to tell him what had happened. He didn't even want to see her. Mrs Hindmarch's eyes were red. It was a miserable week.

Even school was better than home. Ollie spent Wednesday lunch hour with Hazel, just talking, and it was the best bit of the week. Hazel was all right, different from Melanie and Tracy. You got the impression that she wouldn't blab what you'd just said to the next person she met. Ollie hoped not anyway. She told her about the broken window – she had to tell someone – and about her dad keeping her in her room till she confessed to doing it. The new girl had been shocked.

'Why, Ollie, he's prehistoric! He can't do this to you.'

Ollie thought for one dreadful moment she was going

to cry. She couldn't have borne that, would probably have cried herself.

They were in the playground at the time, standing by the entrance to the science block. It was a fine day and they had walked right round the school grounds talking as they went. As much to comfort Hazel as herself, Ollie said not to worry, she was sure that if she held out long enough her dad would give in. He'd have to believe her, wouldn't he? She didn't know how it had happened and that was that. He had poured scorn on the explanations she had offered. Jets! Hailstones! Boys next door! Who did she think he was? A simpleton? That window had been broken by a sharp instrument applied with force to the centre of the pane. How else could she explain the small hole in the middle, out of which radiated the web of cracks? Forced to examine it Ollie felt bound to agree with him. There was a small hole. He was probably right about how it had been made. She disagreed with him about one important detail. He thought she had done it – from the inside. She knew she hadn't – and was pretty sure the force had been applied from outside.

She had evidence too. After her father had stormed out of the room leaving Ollie to 'think about it', she had got on to her knees below the window, scratched among the carpet pile and found the missing piece of glass. She had a small cut on her middle finger to prove it. Surely, she said to Hazel, if she or anyone else had tapped on the window from the inside the glass would have fallen outwards on to the path below.

'Not necessarily, but probably.'

Hazel's voice had a slight American drawl which Melanie said was phoney but Hazel explained she couldn't help it. It would go soon and she would sound the same as everyone else. She picked up accents very quickly, fortunately. It was grim moving so often and being teased wherever she went just because she sounded different.

'Anyway, Ollie, you haven't said how you think the window got broken. Who could have gotten up to the second floor and done it? Is there a fire escape or anything?'

Ollie shook her head. That was the trouble. She couldn't think of anything which would explain it. She still wondered if the boys next door might be involved, if one of them had a catapult, for instance. She had searched every inch of her room, the carpet, the bed-clothes, the shelves, even the picture rail, in case some small sharp object had landed there.

'Did you hear anything? In the night? You said you thought it might be hailstones, what made you think that?'

Ollie told her about the tapping sound. She didn't tell her about the movement behind the curtains because it made her feel stupid to think about it. She'd told her father, said she'd thought it was ivy and he'd grabbed her arm and hauled her outside, forced her to look up at the window. There was no ivy, no climbing plants at all at the back of the house. And there were no trees with branches close enough to touch the window. It made her feel sick thinking of the expression on his face. He looked at her as if she were a slug or a leather-jacket, one of the pests he despised because they destroyed his vegetables. He'd pushed her away and walked towards the back door. Then he'd turned round, jerked his head and told her to get to her room and stay there. That was the last time he had spoken to her.

'Did you see anything?' Hazel's voice made Ollie jump. Ollie didn't know what to say.

'I-I think we'd better be going in.' People were pushing by them. The bell must have gone.

'OK, but Ollie, we must talk about this some more. It's really interesting.'

That night Ollie decided she would tell Hazel about the movement at the window. She had to speak to someone. It wasn't as if the broken window was the only thing which went wrong. Every day that week there was something, little things. The remains of the Sunday joint went missing. The photograph of Mr Hindmarch receiving the Horticultural Society's Gold Cup for the best garden fell off the wall. When she got home on Wednesday her father was already there. A bundle of cedar logs had fallen on his foot at the pencil factory. There were no bones broken but the doctor had told him to rest it for a couple of days. What's more, a choice Cox's Pippin which he'd been keeping for this year's show, disappeared from the fruit bowl. Ollie got the blame. Her father said that nothing was to be left out. Biscuits were to be counted, large cakes measured. Ollie couldn't be trusted, he was ashamed to say it, but it was a fact.

She looked for Hazel the next day but couldn't find her. It was annoying she wasn't in the same class. On Friday Ollie saw her hurrying along the corridor with a violin under her arm. She said she'd been off the previous day with a tummy bug, couldn't talk now because she was on her way to orchestra, but would see her Monday.

Didn't anyone care that she faced another weekend of prison? On Friday evening Ollie trudged up the drive with her bike. On the way home she had thought about running away, but where would she go? The atmosphere at home hurt her. She didn't show it of course, didn't let them see she was upset, but it was horrible.

To be treated as a liar and a thief, or even worse, as if she didn't exist at all and yet was responsible for everything that went wrong, made her feel rotten inside – made her wonder if she were a liar and a thief. She stood outside, not wanting to go in. Windfall apples lay at her feet. She kicked one and it disintegrated into a cloud of black flies. There wasn't even a cosy chat with her mother to look forward to. Funny how that suddenly seemed attractive. Her father would be sitting there, making sure she went straight up to her room.

He was, his face hidden behind the *Helmswick Record*, his foot supported by a kitchen chair. Mrs Hindmarch did have the kettle on and said quietly to Ollie that she would bring her up a cup of tea as soon as it was ready.

'That's where you're wrong, Mother. There's to be no more waiting hand and foot on our Olwen. She can stand on her own two feet. Go on, hop it.' He lowered the paper briefly. These were the first words he had spoken to her since Saturday. Was this the beginning of the thaw?

It wasn't. She spent Friday evening in her room, doing her homework and making a Plasticine model of her father. She gave him a huge nose, and then made an eagle which swooped down on him from a great height. If he didn't want to be friends, see if she cared.

The thaw when it came was not the kind she envisaged or wanted. On Saturday morning she was woken up roughly by her father shaking her arm.

'Right, get downstairs straightaway and start mopping up. I suppose you'd better get dressed first but be quick about it. Sharp now.' He thrust a bundle of clothes in her arms and left the room.

Half asleep Ollie pulled on jeans and jumper. What on earth was he talking about? Mopping up? What had he planned for her now? Not for the first time she wondered if she were taking part in some absurd pantomime, *Cinderella* for instance.

When she was half-way down the stairs she got a hint of what the trouble was. Through the banisters she saw a stream of water trickling through the hall. Someone had rolled up the strip of carpet that usually lay there and stood it on the stairs. Ollie squeezed by.

The tiled floor of the kitchen looked like the foot bath at Whinrith swimming pool. Her mother and father, in wellingtons, stood by the hall door.

'Here she is. Give her the mop.'

Mr Hindmarch was holding out her wellingtons.

'Give her the mop, I said, and the bucket. No, no, breakfast can wait. Now get started. You caused this mess – not to mention all the wasted food, but we'll see about that later – you clear it up.'

Mrs Hindmarch was crying. Ollie looked at the scene before her, water everywhere, with here and there a green pea or some yellow breadcrumbs floating on the surface. She soon pieced together what had happened. The huge freezer which stood in the corner of the kitchen had defrosted itself. Unless of course she went along with her father's interpretation, which was that Ollie had come down in the middle of the night, switched off the freezer, opened the freezer door and turned on the central heating. He had found the door open when he'd come down to breakfast.

It took Ollie all morning to clear up the mess. Mr Hindmarch forbade Mrs Hindmarch to help her. Ollie lost count of the number of times she filled the bucket and emptied it. It was a cold job and the wet soaked into her clothes as she squeezed the mop or lifted the bucket to the sink. Water dribbled into her wellingtons. She was hungry too.

Lunch was late and she ate it alone in her bedroom.

The thick soup was welcome and so were the chunks of bread. But sitting on the edge of her bed in jeans and several jumpers she still felt cold. Needless to say her father hadn't connected the radiator he had bought at the sale. Neither had he mended the broken window. He had simply fixed a double layer of polythene over it. If you looked you could just see the web of cracks through the grey haze.

Web. She saw again the web at the base of the eldertree, saw the face. Could there be an offended spirit at work? Could that be what she had heard tapping at the window a week ago? She got up. Of course not.

At the bottom of her wardrobe there were piles of boxes, presents from years ago. Some of the games were hardly used, but they needed several players. However she had unearthed several old furry toys. They could play if she took their turns. Here was just the thing, a pink and grey donkey, velvety now only between its legs.

She was playing Monopoly with the donkey and a rather repulsive rubbery creature like a squashed human being with lots of black hair, when her mother crept into the room on Sunday evening.

'Ollie love, I'm not really going behind your dad's back, because I've been careful not to promise anything, not to say anything at all, not to agree or disagree, and . . . because . . . and . . . I'm not saying what I think now because . . . well, I don't know what to think to tell you the truth. Anyway' – she took a deep breath and glanced behind her as if she expected to see Mr Hindmarch coming up the stairs – 'your dad's out, a bird-meeting, and I've got a lovely fire in grate and . . . and I'd like you to come downstairs and enjoy it.'

She had even turned the television off, so that she

would hear the car when it came up the drive. Ollie said she thought it would be better to keep the telly on with the sound down. Her mum could turn it up when they heard the car, and she would have some idea what was on and be able to talk about it as she usually did, when her dad came home.

Ollie curled up in an armchair by the fire which snickered and snapped and gently hissed. Purple and creamy-orange flames licked the ashy surface of the logs and the sides of the grate. Tiny purple flames danced round the logs' black centre. A shower of crimson sparks burst from a log and shot up the chimney, one or two sparks lingering in the soot at the back of the fireplace. Ollie watched them vanish one by one. Her mother came in with a tray – tea and Ollie's favourite, chocolate cake with fudgy icing.

'Lovely fire, wind's in right direction for once.' She filled two mugs. 'Mind you, I didn't think these logs would burn so well. Still a bit green, I think, best to let them stand a while really. Here, Ollie, take hold of this, Ollie.'

Ollie was staring at the logs in the hearth. 'Elder branch brought into the house brings . . . ghosts . . . the devil.'

Stop! But the more she stared the more she saw faces in them. Eyes, one pair like an owl's stared back at her. A pair of large lobed ears listened. A creature with horns and a long snout and cavernous nostrils faced the room with a hideous grin. The more she looked the more faces she saw. And not just faces, the gnarled and knotted branches twisted and writhed, with spikes like witches' fingers. A strange animal with jagged claws opened a huge mouth to reveal black entrails. Dead elder. Dreadelder. Ollie knew she was looking at elder logs, knew her imagination had again taken over, knew that the hollows like skull sockets were knot-holes, that the scaly skin was tree bark, that the rough fur was moss. She knew it – and could stop herself.

'Thanks, Mum.' She took the tea. 'Dad still worried about peregrine falcons, is he?'

'Yes, love, they've got someone from Shropshire come to talk to them about a twenty-four-hour watch next year. Says it's the only way to protect the nest from poachers. You and your dad were such mates last spring. Spent a lot of time together watching the nest, didn't you?'

'Yes.' It seemed a long time ago. Why had things suddenly gone wrong?

'I'm sure this . . . er . . . difficulty will all blow over, love.'

'Hope so.'

The fire purred in the grate. There was nothing evil about it. It was a comfortable, comforting sound. Her mother sat in the chair opposite. Ollie stretched her toes, soaked up the warmth. On the television screen a fat woman sang soundlessly, her arms outstretched, then above her head, then clutching her thighs. Ollie laughed. It was nice being down here with her mum. Funny that she wasn't talking non-stop as she usually did when they were alone. She had picked up some knitting, a cardigan it looked like.

'Pass me the pattern, love, it's in that copy of *Woman's Way*, look, there in the magazine rack. By the side of your chair.'

Ollie looked down. And there It was. It. The Thing. Behind the rack. Eyes gleaming and sort of grinning. Carefully Ollie reached for the magazine and handed it to her mother.

'Thank you, love. It'll be nice this. I'm making it for your father for Christmas, a surprise like.'

It was quite obvious that her mother hadn't seen it. Ollie stood up, saw it dart towards the door, beckon. She put her cup on the table.

'I think I'll go to bed, Mum. It's been nice, but I wouldn't like Dad to find me here. You'd get into awful trouble.'

It was waiting at the top of the first flight of stairs, claws gripping the step, bright eyes alert. When it saw she was following, it turned and half crawled, half flew up the second flight of stairs, across the landing and into her bedroom.

Chapter 6

She followed and shut the door behind her. Stood with her back against it, her eyes scanning the room. She heard a snigger but couldn't see the creature. Sniffed. The room smelt different. Woody. Then she saw its reflection in the mirror. It was on the bed, pillow end, half hidden by the brown patterned cover. She turned to look. Her heart was thudding but she couldn't not look, as she couldn't not have followed it.

So this was a bogle. It was brown, several shades of brown, and if she had passed it in Whinlatter Woods she probably wouldn't have noticed. Its skin was dry and rough like the bark of trees, its pointed nose like a knotty twig. It sat on the bed, hugging its knees. At least she supposed they were knees; they were pointed and sort of hinged and bent in the middle. It leaned forward almost folded double, its feet stuck out in front of it like a frog's.

'Ten neets past it weren't dree.' The voice was brittle and crackly, like autumn leaves, the accent broad like farmers high up the fells.

'Pardon?'

'Skin. Dree. Thoo said my skin were dree.'

'I didn't, I only . . .' Ollie stopped; she was going to say 'thought it'.

'Ten neets past it were as ploshed as Brigglebog.' The voice rasped from deep inside its body. 'Ten neets past when I were a-tapping on yon window . . .'

So that was it.

'I didn't know it was you.' Ollie's voice was surprisingly clear.

There was a sound like wood splitting. Its feet clawed the air and its body shook. It was laughing, as if it were never going to stop. The laughter grew louder and it started to throw itself around the bed, turning somersaults and just stopping itself from falling off the edge.

'Stop it! STOP IT! And tell me what you want.'

The strange cracking sound carried on for several moments more, but Ollie could see that it had heard her. It threw a glance in her direction before tossing its head back again.

'Don't!'

It stayed silent, settled itself on the bed like a hen smoothing ruffled feathers.

'I'm sorry.' She regretted shouting. It looked as if it were sulking. Besides her shouting was just as likely to bring her mother upstairs, as its laughter. 'I'm sorry, it's just that . . . just that . . .' She didn't really know what to say.

'Thoo didn't know it were me . . . ha.' Its voice was scornful, and Ollie thought it was going to laugh again.

'Didn't want to know . . . didna didna . . .' Its voice tailed off and the room was silent except for her own breathing and then a scratching sound from the bed.

Slowly Ollie moved forward, lowered herself till her face was level with the bed, watched, as with long pointed fingers, it picked tiny pieces of mud from between its toes and piled them up beside it, ignoring her. She would have to get rid of those before her mother came up. So this was a bogle. Was it male or female? Hard to tell. She would need to turn it upside down to see.

'On no thoo don't.' It hadn't even looked at her, but

there it was again reading her thoughts. 'Wouldna find oot if thoo did. I'm not a furry "pet".' It spat out the word.

It wasn't. It hadn't got fur; it had scaly bark which moved like the plates of an armadillo, except that Ollie had never seen an armadillo, so she couldn't be sure about this. It carried on picking its toes, ignoring her or seeming to while she wondered what to do. She would like to have stopped thinking altogether since she didn't like the thing knowing what went on inside her head, but she knew that was impossible. She'd often tried it when she was worried, and it didn't work. You absolutely had to think of something, and the thought that you didn't want to think had an annoying habit of sliding in, even when you were determinedly thinking of something else. Besides she had to think of what to do. It was looking at her. Saw her looking and turned back to its toes. What should she do? Deep inside herself she knew it was angry because her father had destroyed its home and that she hadn't stopped him, though how it expected her, a mere girl, to stop a grown man from doing what he wanted she did not know.

'Ssssss . . . Ssssss . . .'

At first she thought it was simply hissing, but when she listened more carefully she noticed that the hissing came in short bursts and was in fact made up of words. Straining to hear more she made out a rhyme:

> 'To fazarts
> Hard hazards
> Are death ere they come.
>
> To fazarts
> Hard hazards
> Are death ere they come.'

'Mere girl! Futt!' It made a sound like a small firework exploding. 'Mere girl!' It threw her a derisive glance and then began to examine its scaly fingers, scraping mud from the claw-like nails of its left hand with its right.

'Futt!'

'It's all right for you, you haven't got my father.' Ollie only thought these words but she might just as well have shouted them aloud. The creature stopped scraping and turned to her.

'Fazart.' That word again. What did it mean?

'Thoo has a tongue, hasn't thee? Couldn't thee tell tha father why he shouldna cut down my tree? Couldn't thee tell him what thoo saw, what thoo heard, what thoo felt?'

Ollie closed her eyes, felt again the elderberry stinging her cheek. She had tried. She had told her father that he shouldn't cut the tree down, but no one could stop Albert Hindmarch when he was determined to do something. No one. What was the point of telling him about an elder bogle?

'Thoo's got to.'

Ollie opened her eyes. 'What?'

'Stop him.'

'How?'

'Towp it.'

Towp it? What? It would be easier if it used words she understood.

'Towp the poison. Rid it.'

Ollie's stomach began to whirl. She could hide it yes, but what about her father, when he went to get it and it wasn't there? What about his temper? No, she shook her head; she couldn't do it.

'Fazart. Fazart.' It was jeering at her, calling her that silly name again.

Now the stupid rhyme.

'To fazarts
Hard hazards
Are death ere they come.

To fazarts . . .'

'Shut up, I mean be quiet, I want to think.'

'Krrrrh.' It sounded like a man clearing his throat. Ollie looked down but it was no longer beside her.

'Krrrh.' It was crouching on the dressing-table holding something, a china figure of a girl with a cat on her knee. Ollie loved it.

'Give me that, please.'

It sniggered. She approached slowly, hand outstretched, and just as she reached it, the bogle dropped the figure on the floor. It broke in three pieces. Furious, she snatched at the creature. Too late again. She raced about the room, longed to get her hands on it, ached to choke the creature till there was no life left. How dare it come into her life like this ruining everything?

'Krrh.' From the top of the wardrobe this time. She made a grab. Stopped. What was it holding now? A large square mirror, and it was quite obvious the malicious creature intended to drop it!

'NO!'

'Fazart.' It spoke softly but its voice was full of menace. Lifting its left claw from the mirror it casually scratched its nose.

Diamond-shaped, the mirror swung slowly from side to side, one corner between the creature's claws.

'Don't. Please.'

It was listening she could tell.

'I'll do what you want.'

Its head was slightly cocked to one side.

'I'll do what you want.' She had to convince it. It was quite clear that things would go wrong till she did.

Watching, she waited. From below she could hear the fanfare that announced the ten o'clock news. The fanfare ended, the voice of the announcer began, and to her great relief she saw the bogle slowly stretch out its left claw, lift the hanging corner of the mirror and draw it towards the top of the wardrobe. Then stop.

'Anything?' it asked in its throaty voice.

'Anything.'

There was a clatter as the mirror landed on the top of the wardrobe and a thump as the bogle hit the floor beside her.

Ollie looked down. It was staring up at her.

'Anything?'

Feeling sick in her stomach, she nodded.

'Yan, rid me of the poison.'

It was the old Cumbrian way of counting.

'Tyan, find me a new home. Tethera . . .' It paused as if it needed to think of a third task for her to perform.

Ollie felt sicker. 'How many?'

For answer it stuck its nose in the air. New home? She supposed it meant another eldertree.

'Reet. Like the old 'un. Bushy. 'Ollow. With sap. Quick.'

It had twisted round and was pointing to the scales on its back. 'Look.'

Ollie moved closer. She saw a bare patch.

'Dree. Needs sap.'

As she watched a woody scale fell to the floor.

The creature was drying out. Drying? Dying? Wouldn't that be the end to her problems? She glanced at its face, was held by its bright eyes, and she felt her own face burn.

It looked tired now. She saw its mouth open, heard a creaky yawn. And then it was saying something.

'Wintersleep. Sap then sleep. Hollow tree to hide.'

She would do what it said. Find it a home. Get rid of the poison, and – three things it had said – whatever else it asked. Her father, well she'd just have to hope. It was speaking again. What now?

'Elder black love lack. Elder white love bright.'

She waited but it said no more. Well, she'd start tomorrow. An eldertree and somewhere to hide the poison. Or should she just pour it away? She looked down to see what it thought. But it wasn't there. She searched the room but found only a woody scale beside her bed. She picked it up. Picked up too the broken pieces of the girl with the cat, wrapped them in a handkerchief and put them in the dressing-table drawer.

Chapter 7

She woke early and wondered why. Remembered – and dismissed the idea. It had been a dream, that was all, a bad dream. She tried to go back to sleep, but her shoulders were stiff and her stomach surged, urging her to be doing something. Silly. She turned over, and gritty mud fell from the bedcover on to the carpet. Oh. Leaning over, she scraped as much as she could under the bed, then got up. The broken ornament was in the drawer, and so was the woody scale.

What had it said? 'One, get rid of the poison. Towp it.' Towp? Anyway, she must start. She put on her shoes. The house was quiet. She crept on to the landing and listened at her parents' door, thought she could hear steady breathing. Tiptoed downstairs. The kitchen was shadowy, sun leaking through the thin curtains. A tap dripped, clanging in the sink. The door key clunked as she turned it. She waited, straining her ears for sounds from above, opened the door and went out.

A hen squawked as she neared the bottom of the garden, thrusting its beak through the wire netting on the henhut window. She opened the shed door. There it was, the can of sodium chlorate, just inside. Carrying it down the path, she looked up. So far so good. No one along the ridge was up yet. All the bedroom curtains were closed anyhow.

Round the front, too, curtains were closed. Quick as she could now, down to the bottom of the drive, trying to tread softly on the slate chips. She pushed the can beneath the laurel bush by the gate, made sure it was completely hidden by the broad waxy leaves. Back to bed now. She would collect it later.

But what was that? Hand on the door she froze. Then realized. The alarm clock. But it was no good standing outside. She opened the door. There was movement upstairs. She glanced down – wet shoes. How to explain them? How to explain being in the kitchen? Idea. She filled the kettle, plugged in, then wiped her shoes on the kitchen towel, wiped the floor too. Re-locked the door. Cups now. The hall door opened.

'So that's where you are. Well hop it, and get dressed.'

'I-I thought I'd bring you and Mum a cup of tea in bed.'

'Well don't. We're up. Hop it, I said. It'll take more than a cup of tea to put right the damage you've done.'

It could have been worse. At least he went off to work early. She breakfasted with her mum, said goodbye when Doris the postlady came in, retrieved the can from beneath the bush, hid it in a plastic bag, fixed it to her bike, and set off for school.

What was she looking for? A hiding place for the can, and a hibernating place for the bogle, an eldertree, a bushy one with plenty of sap it had said. Neither task should be that difficult. There was nothing but countryside between here and Helmswick and elderberry was very common. Must be lots of hiding places, lots of eldertrees.

So why couldn't she see either? She was pedalling so slowly that she almost fell off. Maybe she ought to have taken the back road and not the main one. Traffic was heavy and it was dangerous not concentrating fully. But she had to look and she couldn't walk into school with a can of poison. Trouble was, the sides of the roads were so tidy. No hedges. There was a grass verge, recently mown, then a wire fence with a neat ditch the other side. No hedges or walls. No long grass. Nowhere to hide anything.

'Beep. B – eep!' A lorry hurtled past, followed by the school bus, faces pressed to the window at the back, some waving hands. She couldn't wave back.

Why hadn't she seen a single elderberry tree? The bright orange berries of the rowan were everywhere. She began to wonder if trees moved around the countryside at night. When she wanted conkers there were never any chestnut trees. Already houses were in sight, the outskirts of Helmswick. Where could she put the can? It would have to be that litter bin on the other side of the road. She got off her bike, managed to cross over, looked over her shoulder and dropped the can into the bin.

It was nearly nine o'clock; she was worried. It wasn't going to be as easy as she thought. The turning for school was only a short way off. Hundreds of grey uniforms, some on bikes, were converging on the large gateway. One or two teachers passed in their cars. Where was Hazel? Melanie's mother drove away in her Mercedes and there was Melanie. Pushing her bike down the drive Ollie examined the trees growing on either side, beech mostly, behind them a privet hedge and here and there a hollybush.

In the classroom she was surprised to see Hazel at the front.

'New class. From today. The reports from my other school have arrived . . .'

At this point Burridge came in and gloom descended. It wasn't till break that they had a proper talk.

Ollie told Hazel everything. It was a risk but she had

to take it. She needed help. To her relief Hazel didn't giggle. Nor was she excessively kind in a way that would have proved to Ollie that she thought she was mad. She was simply intensely curious.

'Go on, Ollie, go on. This tallies with lots that I know about North American Indians. They believe in tree spirits you know.'

Together they searched the school grounds. They searched them again during the dinner hour. There was a growth of elder near the caretaker's house but it could hardly be called a bush let alone a tree. Ollie despaired.

'There isn't any. I told you. It's as if they've all disappeared in the night.'

'Don't be daft. I've seen hundreds.'

'So did I think I'd seen hundreds.'

'Farmers are always complaining of it . . .'

'Yes and they're ripping it up along with the rest of the hedges.'

Hazel was still optimistic. 'You take the back road home tonight. I'll search Scawthwaite. You can't tell me there isn't a single eldertree between our two homes.'

Ollie pushed her bike home and examined every tree along the route. There was not one eldertree. It seemed impossible, but it was true. There was oak, ash and alder, their leaves just beginning to take on their autumn colouring. There was spruce and Douglas fir. There were blackberry bushes trying to force their way through the dry stone wall, old man's beard frothing over the wall tops, and rowan trees, bright against the grey-green landscape – but not a single elder.

She fought off despair. Hazel would think she was wet if she gave up now. Several roads converged on the village. How much time had she got? It was 4.45. She checked the ridge. No sign of her father's car in the drive. Perhaps he was doing overtime. She pedalled past. With luck she could look up Newlands Road and get home in time. She soon had to get off as it was a steep climb. There were hedges here, and trees, but not one of them was elder. She raced down the hill, thinking frenziedly. Where now? It was 5.15. Better check that her dad wasn't home.

He wasn't so she searched the campsite opposite. It was the same story. No eldertrees. She searched the banks of the beck as far as Cartmer's Farm. Hawthorn, blackberry, willow, ash, more hawthorn. It was the same all along except for one stretch which was completely bare, where everything had been uprooted, and the bank had been reinforced with large stones and wire netting.

When she reached home at six she was near to tears, hardly caring if her father were there or not. She'd failed. The future looked bleak – and he was there looking at his watch.

'What time do you call this, madam? Bed. But first get down the garden and fetch an egg for your mother. Sharp about it.'

She went but walked slowly, listening and looking all about her, miserable at her failure. Scared too. What would happen next? Where was the bogle now? How quickly did it expect her to perform the tasks? What would it do if she didn't?

The toolshed door was closed. Behind the shed stood the hollow elder stump, like a rotten tooth. Otherwise nothing, nothing unusual that is. Trees stirred, hens clucked and three of them came to the wire thinking she had brought food. Ollie stepped back to the vegetable garden, tore off some cabbage leaves and threw them into the run. Two more hens appeared. The sixth must have gone broody, would be fluffed up in a nesting box inside the coop. Ollie removed the padlock that fastened the hen-coop door, placed it on the low roof, ducked and stepped inside.

Her scream must have brought her father because he was holding her when she came round. She was outside the coop with her head between her knees and she felt terrible. She began to cry. Her mother was there too stroking Ollie's forehead and dabbing her eyes, saying, 'Oh dear, oh dear,' over and over again. When the ground stopped surging up to meet her, and the hen-house stopped spinning, Ollie opened her eyes, but kept them focused on her knees which were grazed and streaked with mud and chicken droppings. She felt sick, but sicker as she recalled the scene inside the henhouse.

'Best get you inside, lass. Must have tripped and hit your head when you rushed out.' It was her dad's voice, gruff but kind. She felt herself lifted high as he picked her up and carried her back to the house. By the time they reached the kitchen she was struggling to be free.

'I'm all right now. Honest.'

He sat her down on a chair near the table. Her mother was filling the kettle. 'You keep an eye on her, Mother, I'll go and sort things out down yonder.'

Ollie knew what he was going to do, though it was too late. The hen had been dead hanging there, a nail through its neck, red-black blood a solid trickle over its bronze feathers. She began to cry again.

'It's all right, love.' Her mother had cotton wool and was bathing her head. 'It's all right now, it was a horrid sight, but no one's blaming you, even your dad knows you couldn't have done that.'

But Ollie did blame herself and when she got to her bedroom after tea she saw that something else also blamed her. On the window-sill in letters formed of tiny twigs was one word: 'FAZART'.

Chapter 8

It wasn't fair. She'd tried. Tried hard to do what it had said. Had got rid of the poison. Or had she? What was that? Outside her father was striding down the garden path, and he had a can in his right hand. It looked familiar. It could be petrol for the mower of course but it looked like . . .

'Stop! STOP!'

She went to bang on the window, then remembered it was broken. No point shouting either. He couldn't hear.

She raced downstairs. Was it sodium chlorate he was carrying? How could he have got hold of it? Surely he hadn't bought another one already. When did he discover it had gone? She rushed past her mother, opened the kitchen door and ran down the garden.

'Stop!' She was too breathless to say anything else. Her father looked up. He was unscrewing the cap.

'Stop, please.'

She expected him to rant and rave, or at least be very sarcastic, but he didn't. He just looked at her for what seemed like several minutes, then started to screw the cap on. Crikey, this was too easy! He was saying something too.

'And I've taken . . . it down . . .' He nodded his head in the direction of the henhouse. '. . . and buried it. I thought you'd like that. It's near them marigolds.'

'Thanks.'

'I've worked out how it happened. There was a nail sticking out, I've been meaning to bang it in for ages, hen must have caught itself on it when it were flying up to its perch. Chance in a million. Couldn't have done it, if it had tried.' He carried the can into the shed and came out again. 'Funny that, I could swear I'd put another one there. Must be in the garage. No.' He looked up at the sky. 'It looks like rain again, I wouldn't have thought of doing it tonight, only I saw Fred Tyrell on the dustcart, and he said he'd found this full can in one of the bins and asked if I could be doing with it.'

So that was it.

'I don't want you to do it at all.'

'What?'

'Kill the tree.'

'Oh.' He looked at the stump. 'There's not a lot left of it to kill, is there?'

There wasn't. If it grew again, even without the sodium chlorate on the remains of its roots, it would be a miracle.

'Are you going to though? Finish it off I mean, with that stuff?'

He shook his head. 'I don't know, Olwen. Mebbe, mebbe not. I'll wait and see. I'm making no promises now.' He put the spade in the shed. 'Why does it matter so much anyhow?'

She couldn't tell him even though he was being kind. He probably thought she was bonkers already. If she told him he'd be convinced. The hens were making soft crooning sounds from their perches. They'd decided it was bedtime. Mr Hindmarch went and closed the hen-hole.

'Must keep fox out. Time we went in too. It's nearly eight o'clock. And you shouldn't be rushing about, after a knock like that.'

She had some maths homework so she went up to her room. The twigs on the window-sill were in a heap. Had she piled them up? She couldn't remember. She had stopped her father, for tonight anyway. It ought to be pleased. Maybe it was. Where was it? Again she looked round the room. There was no point in summoning it; she knew that now; it did what it wanted, came and went as it pleased. Why couldn't it find itself a home?

Determination fought with despair. She would find an eldertree. She couldn't find an eldertree. Wouldn't, couldn't. Would could. Goodwood. She would. She had to find an eldertree.

Downstairs the phone rang. She heard her mother answering it. 'Lanthwaite 703 . . . hello . . . who? . . . Oh I don't know . . .' She looked over the banisters, saw her mum dithering by the phone, her hand covering the receiver. Catching sight of Ollie she beckoned her down. 'It's a Mrs Jehu, says she's the mother of a friend of yours called Hazel, wants you to go and have tea tomorrow night . . . I don't know . . .'

'You'd better ask Dad.' Why couldn't her mother make some decisions on her own? Ollie didn't hold out much hope, but here was her mother smiling.

'Mrs Jehu? Yes, that will be all right. Thank you very much. Would you like . . . oh, you'll bring her home . . .All right then, yes I'll write a letter to the headmistress. Thank you very much . . . Oh would she, all right then, yes, she's standing here now. Hazel wants to speak to you, Olwen.'

Ollie grabbed the phone. They both spoke together.

'Hazel, have you . . .?'

'Ollie, I've found one!'

She could only mean one thing. Afterwards Ollie

bounded upstairs and was in her room dancing with the pink donkey when her mum walked in.

'Oh.'

'Come in, Mum. What is it?'

She started straightening the bedclothes.

'What is it, Mum? What do you want to say?'

She was smoothing the pillow now. 'Just your dad, love, don't expect him to say sorry, but he is. He thinks he may have been a bit harsh. 'Night love, I'll go and write that letter now, so you can have a place on the school bus to Hazel's. Your dad'll give you a lift to school.'

Ollie walked over to the window-sill. It was dark outside. She thought of September as a summery month but the days were really quite short. It was good news about the tree though, and about going to Hazel's, and about her dad being sorry. If only the bogle would be patient.

It wasn't. Next morning Ollie was in the back of the car on the way to school when her bag lurched towards the door. Mr Hindmarch saw her scared face in the mirror but fortunately thought it was his fault.

'No need to look like a frightened rabbit, Olwen. It's not you I'm mad at. Bloody poachers, that's who.' He tapped the copy of *Bird Watcher* on the seat beside him. 'Bloody stupid judge.'

They'd stopped behind a lorry now, couldn't pass because of the traffic in the other direction, and the bag jumped again, towards her this time. 'Twenty-five quid! What's twenty-five quid to the likes of them? An invitation to come back next year. I bet they laughed in his face.'

Ollie watched the bag. It was perfectly still. Must have been the movement of the car.

'Where was this, Dad?'

'Scotland.'

'Ouch!' The bag crashed into her side – and the car wasn't moving!

'What's up?' He was looking at her.

'Nothing.' She tried to think of something else to say. There were sounds now which she didn't want him to hear. 'Well at least they caught them, Dad.'

'What's that you said?'

'The poachers – in Scotland, the police caught them. The ones who stole our eggs got away.'

'Oot.'

'Shut up. How much do you get for a peregrine egg, Dad? Shut up.'

'Difficult to say, exact, hundreds anyhow.'

'OH!'

The 'oots' were getting louder. She tried hard to speak over them and stop her school bag jumping up and down. Fortunately the traffic started moving again and the noise of the engine helped – a bit.

'Oot! Oot!'

'What was that you said, Olwen?'

'Nothing.' She tried hard to hold the bag down. 'I mean nothing much. Just that it's nearly time to get OUT.'

'OOT! OOT!'

The cries were so loud he must be deaf not to hear them.

She was shouting herself: 'IT'S NEARLY QUARTER TO NINE. NICE DAY THOUGH. NOT RAINING. A BIT WINDY PERHAPS. LOOK AT THE LEAVES FALLING OFF THE TREES.' She knew she sounded like an imbecile but it was difficult making conversation while clinging to a bag that was trying to jump out of a moving car.

'Are you all right, Ollie?' Help, he was looking over

his shoulder. 'I said to your mother we ought to have let a doctor have a look at you. How's your head?'

'FINE. It's fine. I'm fine. Thanks.' The thing had quietened down and she caught sight of herself in the mirror, arms clutching the bag, face bright red. When they reached the school gates she nearly fell from the car in her eagerness to be out, ran for cover behind the trees.

'Now just listen, you.' She knelt down and undid the zip. There was silence and all she could see were books. 'I'm doing my best. If you carry on like that you'll ruin everything.'

Silence. Or did something stir in the darkness at the bottom? Something whizzed by her ear and landed about a metre away. She heard laughter behind her.

'Gotcha!'

'Wotcha doing, Hindmarch?'

'BEhindmarch!'

This caused hysterical laughter. Some boys Ollie didn't know could hardly stand up with laughing.

'I know what she's doing.' It was Melanie Laxton's super-drone. 'Oh, Ollie, I *do* think you could have waited. It's not that far to the bogs.'

Fits of laughter this time. More boys gathered and some girls. Ollie stood up, laughed herself, and loathed Melanie Laxton.

She was late, and as she walked in Burridge was sentencing the class to break picking up litter.

'All except you, Olwen. You can do it today *and* tomorrow.'

With a triumphant smirk she sat down – and farted.

The class exploded. Burridge stood up looking furious, then with a 'you can't fool me' expression, reached behind her for the whoopee cushion – which wasn't there. She sat down again, and again made a very rude noise. The class roared.

'Right who was it? I can take a joke as well as anyone but if that happens again you will all be kept in after school.'

Fortunately there was silence, except for whispered discussions as to who could have done it. Jason Smith pretended to faint as if the smell was too much for him – there was a rotten pong – and she made him stand outside the door. He breezed out, making exaggerated gestures of great relief, gulping in the fresh air from outside the door.

'Close the door, Jason!' She took a red biro from her handbag. Creep Melanie made a show of picking up a chewing-gum paper from under Jason's desk and putting it in the waste-paper basket.

'Thank you, Melanie. Now class, silence while I take the register. Silence. I said. Silence. Er . . .' The biro she'd been holding had gone, though she'd had it only seconds before. Ollie watched her lift the register and look beneath it, move the board rubber, move a pile of exercise books, look into her bag again.

Ollie looked into her bag which was on the floor beside her. She took out all the books. It was empty. Could it . . .? She looked around the classroom. There was no sign of the bogle. But Burridge's red biro was on Melanie Laxton's desk! And Melanie had just belched and Burridge had seen her pen. Ollie could see her brain working. Melanie! Not Melanie. It must have been someone else, but she was the only one who had been near her desk, when she'd been putting the chewing-gum paper in the basket. She must have done it. A joke that's what it was. Melanie had made a joke. Well, she could take a joke. Ollie watched her composing her features into a smile, turning her mouth up at the ends.

'All right Melanie, bring it here.'

'What, Miss Burridge?'

The smile sagged. Burridge pointed. Melanie saw the pen and looked as if it were going to spring at her. 'It wasn't me, miss.'

'It wasn't me.'

'Here. I'm waiting. Now.'

Melanie's hand hovered over the pen. 'Honestly.'

'NOW!' The bell went for assembly. 'And WHAT is that you've got on your face?'

As Melanie crossed the room, the whole class could see sooty rings circling her eyes. She looked like a racoon. Except that racoons don't have bright red faces. Even her scalp shone red through her pale hair.

'Make-up is not allowed. You know that. Go and wash it off immediately.'

Burridge. Now Melanie. This was too good to be true. Who next? That sadistic PE teacher with a bit of luck.

But nothing happened in PE. Nothing unusual happened all afternoon. There was a tingle of excitement as the class streamed into the last lesson, maths with Burridge, but they were disappointed. Burridge doled out work and sat down – but there were no rude noises. They all settled down to work. Ollie looked around her, wondered about the bogle. Burridge was picking her nose. Disgusting. She hadn't seen the bogle all day. Had it got her message? How would it get to the bus? She leaned over and made sure the zip on her bag was undone.

Chapter 9

The bogle didn't reveal itself during the lesson. When the bell went Ollie put her books carefully into her bag. It was raining outside so she and Hazel dashed to the bus. Inside, she searched again. The interior lights were on: it seemed dark outside. While Hazel talked to the girl behind her, Ollie rummaged in her bag. No bogle. Nor could she see it on the luggage rack or round her feet.

'Well, do you want one or not?'

It was Jason, opposite, offering her a sweet.

'Oh, thanks.'

'It were great today, weren't it – Burridge grunting I mean.'

Ollie laughed and Hazel turned round, pointing to the window.

'Look at that lot. Have you got a mac or cagoule or something?' It was raining hard, rolling misty rain, blurring the line between sky and mountain, and she had no waterproof, only a blazer.

Dull red lights ahead. The bus stopped; a boy got off, entered a waiting car; the bus started again. It stopped and started at different points along the route, usually in villages, sometimes at the end of a lonely road, where a car or farm truck waited. Still the rain fell.

'Us next. My mother's meeting us.'

They drew up by a signpost saying SCAWTHWAITE 1½ MILES.

The bus drove off. There was no car waiting.

'Sorry about this, Helen should be here.'

Ollie pulled up her collar uselessly.

'My mother I mean, she prefers me to call her that. You too I expect. Look I think it's best if we start walking, she can't miss us, there's only one road.'

Ollie was worried. Didn't like things going wrong. The bogle wasn't patient. Where was the eldertree? All she could see were grey walls, grey sheep, grey mountains, their tops lost in cloud and a long grey road. Water was streaming down her neck.

'Where's this eldertree then?'

'Pattinson's farm, in the village.'

The bag slipped off her shoulder. She stopped to hitch it up.

'Ssssss . . .' Oh no. She tried to think positively. At least it was there. She ran to catch up. 'Hazel, let's go now – to the tree I mean.'

'Sure Ollie, just as soon as we get there.'

It was moving around, knocking against her side. They walked faster, spray spattering their legs.

'Is the tree before the house or after?'

'After.'

'Let's go to the tree first anyway. How far now?'

'About half a mile. Try not to worry, Ollie.'

Ollie felt sick.

'Ssssss . . .' She could hear it over the rain. Surely Hazel could too? It was more than hissing. 'Fazart.' That word again; it meant trouble. 'Fazart.'

'Stop, Hazel, listen.'

They stopped but it went quiet. All they could hear was the sound of water streaming down the fell sides.

So they pressed on, running as much as they could, wet clothes clinging to them. Ollie was desperately worried. Things were going wrong. Very wrong. The bogle was angry. Her clothes would be ruined, her parents furious – and Hazel didn't understand.

'There it is.' At last! Ollie looked but it wasn't the tree. It was a barn-like building standing on its own. The village was still ahead of them.

'And there's Helen, typical, look, in the garage, the car must have broken down again.' A small figure, red hair like Hazel's, straightened up as the engine roared into action.

'Hello there!' She rushed to open the front door.

'Hazel, the tree, *please*!'

'Oh Ollie, ten minutes won't make any difference.'

'Come in. Come in. Oh you poor darlings, it was the stupid carburettor. Do come inside and get your wet clothes off.'

'Hazel, PLEASE!' Ollie could have hit her.

She was simply following her mother into the house where a large collyish dog bounded at them. 'Down Cerby, down.' They both laughed and tickled him.

'HAZEL!' Ollie nudged her, hard.

'Helen, by the way Ollie and I must go outside . . .'

'Yes, darlings, of course, but later; you must get into some dry things. Now, yes, Hazel, you go to my room and use the bathroom there. Olwen, Ollie, what shall I call you, do call me Helen, come upstairs and I'll show you the bathroom. Get out of the way, Cerberus.' He was lying across the stairs. Hazel had disappeared. 'Take off your uniform, have a hot shower or better still a bath, and slip on the bathrobe hanging on the door, I expect we can find you some slippers too. And don't worry about your own clothes, I shall have those dry in no time. Stick them outside the door. Right? I'll go down and put the kettle on.'

What could she *do*? Ollie closed the bathroom door. Stood with hands clenched, stared at a flowery bath in the middle of the room. She heard footsteps running up the stairs and a knock on the door. Mrs Jehu's voice.

'Ollie, tea or coffee or something else? And would you like it in there?'

'Er, er . . . tea please.' Pause. Footsteps going down. What could she do? More footsteps.

'It's outside the door.'

'Thank you.'

What on earth could she do?

Feeling a fool, she spoke to the bag. 'Wherever you are you'll have to wait.' Then she turned on the taps and took off her wet clothes, put them on the landing, picked up her tea, locked the door and climbed into the warm water. Any other time it would have been bliss.

'But when can we go?' They were in the kitchen. Ollie watched her clothes in the tumble-drier. Hazel was tickling the dog again and telling him he was a dumple-wumple. Mrs Jehu had gone to her study to write up case-notes. She was a doctor, Hazel said. There was no sign of the bogle.

'When? And don't tell me not to worry. Where exactly is this tree?'

'Along the High Street, past the pub; turn left. Big black gates.'

'Well, let's get dressed and go.'

'Ollie, have you looked out of the window?'

The rain seemed solid now. They had to press their faces against the glass to see it. Water was running off the fells, streaming towards the house, swirling round the sides of the building.

'It's grim out there, Ollie. It wouldn't like it. You said it didn't like being – what was the word it used – ploshed? Think about it. It knows you're trying, it must do. Wasn't it great at school today, embarrassing all the people you can't stand? I think it's cute.'

Cute! She made it sound like a cuddly toy or a daft dog!

'It's not a pet, Hazel, it said so, and it may have seemed to be on my side today, but it won't last. You know it won't. When it thinks I'm not doing what it wants something bad happens. Something awful . . . oh!'

Ollie realized she hadn't told Hazel about the dead hen. When she did Hazel went quiet.

'Well? What do you think now?'

Still Hazel said nothing.

'What are you thinking? It's obvious you're thinking something, so tell me.'

Hazel walked away. 'No, Ollie, I had a thought but it's irrelevant, nothing to do with this at all.'

'Hazel!' Ollie was furious. How dare she treat her like this! 'Tell me!'

'No, Ollie, it's crazy . . .'

'TELL ME!' Ollie grabbed her wrist.

'All right. All right.' She spoke fast as if it wasn't important at all. 'In some countries but not England, a dead chicken is a sign, an omen, that's all . . .'

'Meaning?'

'Oh, it's all bound up with voodoo, superstitious rubbish, and it's got nothing to do with this, I'm certain. Look, I wish I hadn't told you, stop looking like that.'

But Ollie didn't care what she looked like. She was remembering books she had read, films she had seen, of chicken entrails burning, of graves sliding open and zombies rising from the dead. A dead chicken was an omen of death.

'No one's got it in for you, Ollie.'

Oh no?

'Ollie.' Hazel was shaking her arm. 'You said yourself, your father's been nicer to you since the chicken incident.'

He had but . . .

'And, honestly, Burridge is no worse to you than anyone else. Come on, Ollie, get a grip.'

Ollie looked up. Hazel was smiling. Ollie couldn't.

'I want to go. Now. And if you won't come I'll go by myself.'

The door opened. 'Oh there you are, girls.' It was Mrs Jehu. 'Good, that thing's stopped.' She opened the tumble-drier. 'And they're dry, Ollie.'

'Thank you.' Ollie took them from her and raced upstairs. Rain or no rain, with or without Hazel, she was going to find that tree. There was time before dinner. Must be, there was no sign of it yet. She would get dressed, go downstairs, ask for a mac and OUT. If they thought she was crazy, so what? She wouldn't feel better till she'd found a winter home for the bogle. Dressing, she announced to the bathroom, 'I'm going. Now.' She grabbed her bag. Said it again when she was out on the landing.

Hurrying downstairs she rehearsed what she would say. 'Could you lend me a mac and some wellingtons, please? I really must go for a walk before dinner.'

Right, deep breath, open kitchen door.

'Could . . .'

'Ah, here she is, here's Ollie.' A bearded man with bulging grey eyes stepped forward, shook Ollie's hand.

'Ollie, Peter, Peter, Ollie.' Helen was at the oven. Hazel was laying the table.

'A drink, Ollie?' Mr Jehu was handing her a glass. 'Apple juice, I made it myself.'

Say no thank you. Say I want to go out.

'I'd really like . . .'

A cry from Helen bearing a brown dish.

'Out of the way. Out of the way! Sit down everybody. Abracadabra! Wonders of modern science. Now you don't see it, now you do, dinner in five minutes flat. Praise be to the microwave. Goulash.'

She banged it on the table. They all laughed and sat down but Ollie didn't feel like laughing.

'And baked potatoes!' They looked raw. She felt ill.

All through the meal the Jehus talked. They discussed the wine. They discussed the food. They discussed books and newspapers and hospitals and universities. They discussed the time they would take Ollie home and who would take her. Dr Jehu said she would but not in the Morris. Mr Jehu said he would, as he had to go to a meeting in Whinrith at eight and would drop her off on the way. About 7.40 if that would be all right? Ollie felt sicker. It was already quarter past seven! She kicked Hazel under the table.

'Helen, couldn't Ollie stay a bit longer? We haven't done half the things we planned on doing. Haven't even looked outside yet and it's gone seven. Couldn't you take her home?'

'I could, darling, but I'd rather not. The Morris is not reliable and Peter needs the other car. Look, I have a better idea. Ollie, how would you like to come for the weekend?' Ollie had her mouth full but nodded. Tried to look enthusiastic. What day was it? Tuesday. Would the bogle wait that long?

'That's settled then. I'll ring your mother and fix it, if you're not going away for the weekend or anything?'

Ollie shook her head. They wouldn't be going away for the weekend because they never went anywhere, except to her auntie's and that was only for the day. Funny, that was the first time she'd seen the wretched bogle.

'Eh, Ollie?'

It was Hazel's dad speaking to her. Laughing too. 'I can see you're a dreamer, Ollie.'

The subject had changed. They were talking now about the stone circle just outside Helmswick. Had Ollie been there? Fortunately she had and could tell them a bit about it. It was near to where her father camped when he was guarding the peregrine falcon's nest. Yes, she could take them. That was settled then, they would go at the weekend. A pilgrimage to the magic circle would be made. Mr Jehu's eyes bulged even more. Hazel explained that he was an anthropologist, and got very excited about such things. He hadn't realized that there was a mini-Stonehenge so near to him and was quite delighted at the discovery. He was interested too in her father's bird-watching activities. Very admirable, he called it. Magnificent birds. The Jehus talked and talked and talked, all of them trying to draw Ollie into the conversation, and the more they did, the more out of it Ollie felt.

It had gone wrong. No one understood. She'd thought Hazel did but she didn't. The day was a failure and she didn't look forward to the journey home with Mr Jehu and his interminable questions. What on earth would she say to him?

It was worse than she expected. All the way home Mr Jehu talked, and beside her on the back seat her bag jiggled from side to side. From within came rustling sounds, scratching and scraping. She didn't dare open the zip and longed for the privacy of her own room, but when she got home her mother was keen to talk. Helen had already rung to ask about the weekend and her father was thinking about it. He'd gone off to a bird meeting.

It was 8.30 when she went upstairs to her bedroom

and opened her bag to begin her social studies homework. It was 8.33 exactly when she discovered the full extent of the bogle's anger at her delay. All she could see was its knobbly nose sticking out of a pile of torn-up pieces of paper. She couldn't do her social studies homework because it had torn up her book. It had torn up every book in her bag. She yelled at it, 'You're bad, bad, BAD!' and it replied by snowing her room with paper. When she had cleared it all up Ollie cried herself to sleep.

Chapter 10

Her throat felt sore when the alarm woke her. She switched it off. 5.30. Why? A scrap of paper on the carpet told her. She got out of bed, picked up the paper, checked there was no more, caught sight of her face in the mirror, not red and blotchy thank goodness, just pale and puffy round the eyes. Five minutes later she was in the garden pouring the sodium chlorate into the neighbour's garden. She threw the can over the fence too. It wasn't a brilliant idea – if her father started making inquiries he might discover it – but she couldn't think of a better one.

Back to bed but not to sleep. She was far too worried. Worried wasn't the word. The school day boded nothing but bad. How could she explain why every book in her bag had been torn up? Occasionally someone came to school and said their baby brother or their dog or cat had torn something, but never everything – and she didn't have a dog or a cat or baby brother. So what could she say? And how would she pay for them? She couldn't ask her parents. The last thing she wanted was for them to find out. That would certainly mean no to her weekend at Hazel's.

Blast Hazel. If she'd co-operated this would never have happened. Blast her gabby family. Blast everything. Terrible things could happen before the weekend. She needed to find another eldertree today. And she must hide the fact that she had no books . . .

perhaps tell some teachers she'd lost one . . . hope that they didn't get together and discover that she'd lost them all. Certainly Burridge mustn't find out she'd lost the lot.

A cough from next door. She checked the brown paper bag under the bed. Her mother mustn't find the torn pieces. She'd dump them on the way. Surely Fred Tyrell didn't inspect all the rubbish in the bins before he put it on the dustcart.

She groaned. There was so much to do. If only she could stay in bed. Now if she were ill! If she were ill today then that would put off the evil day till tomorrow . . . but if she were ill tomorrow that would probably be the end of her going to Hazel's for the weekend. And if she didn't go to Hazel's she wouldn't find the tree, and if she didn't find the tree . . . who knows? And if she didn't get up today there was no chance of finding a tree before the weekend.

Her mother was surprised to see her dressed when she opened the bedroom door. 'Turned over a new leaf, Olwen?'

Leaf! Ollie felt her face going red, her blood pounding. It was ridiculous. Why should something as ordinary as that make her feel guilty? Leaf, tree, eldertree. Leaf, turn over a new leaf, take a leaf out of someone's book. Book! Ollie looked at the floor. Perhaps there were some pieces of paper she hadn't seen. When she looked up her mother had already gone downstairs. She told herself not to be stupid. If she stayed as jittery as this she would never be able to cope with the day. She needed all her wits about her.

She didn't find an eldertree on the way to school.

It was maths first lesson. No chance of bluffing here. The old exercise book she had brought with her had lines not squares. The thing to do was act. If she went to her place and sat down she would get nervous, become paralysed, wait to be discovered. So straight to the front. Burridge was reading something.

'Miss Burridge . . .' She saw Ollie and frowned. 'I-I'm afraid my maths book got ruined last night. Could I have another please?'

'Pardon. Speak up. What are you doing out of your seat? Sit down.'

Ollie wondered what to do first. 'I need another maths book . . . please?'

'I said *sit down*. That's better. Now what is it you want?'

Ollie said it again.

'And how did this happen, Olwen?'

'My bag fell off on the way home, into a puddle, some of the books fell out and . . . er . . . a lorry ran over them.'

'Idiot.' Shut up Hazel.

'Oh dear. Fell off your bike, did you say?'

'Yes.' And as she said it Ollie realized she was an idiot. She hadn't gone home on her bike yesterday. Her mother had written to the head asking for permission to go home on the school bus. The question was – did Burridge know?

'I'm surprised your father didn't mention it last night at the Ornithological Society. Ah, I see he hasn't mentioned our mutual membership of the Ornithologists.' She smirked and her gaze held Ollie's. 'Well, Olwen, now you know. It's a very good reason for ensuring that your behaviour in school is . . . er . . . what shall I say . . . impeccable?'

Now Ollie was stuck for words. Burridge and her father knew each other!

'Well, I'd like the money tomorrow. Today you can work on paper. No, no stay in your place. Melanie will bring you some. And when you get your new book, Olwen, you will of course do all the work completed since the beginning of term.'

So far so bad, but at least she hadn't spotted her blunder about the bike. But what about her joining the bird watchers? That was not good news.

In music, surprise surprise, they hadn't needed their books. Skinny Tinny played records. In English Miss Quinn gave her another book and said she must bring in the money as soon as possible and in science when Ollie told Mr Sparrow she couldn't find her book he'd simply said, 'Look harder then, I expect you looked with your nose.'

It was during the afternoon – in French – that things started to go wrong. First of all, instead of Mrs Symien, Burridge walked in, unfurled a plan of a French town and pinned it to the board. *'La ville,'* she said, making it rhyme with 'kill'. 'Copy it into your books then answer the questions which I shall write on the board.'

She scratched away while Ollie wondered what to do. She decided to write in her old book and hope that Burridge would sit down and do some marking.

Burridge didn't sit. When she'd finished at the board she paraded up and down the aisles giving them the benefit of her appalling French accent. Ollie kept her head down and did the work as neatly as she could. She had copied the plan and just begun on the questions when she felt the back of her neck prickle. Her hand stiffened. Burridge was standing behind her.

'Qu'est-ce que c'est?' It came out as a long sucking sound and Ollie didn't understand. But she knew it meant trouble.

'Qu'est-ce que c'est? WHAT IS THAT? I suppose your French book fell out of your bag too and fell into the gutter and got soaking wet?'

'Yes, Miss Burridge.'

'And where did this happen, Olwen?'

It was difficult repeating the lie, knowing it could be proved wrong but she hadn't any choice.

'On the Helmswick road, before the Lanthwaite turn.'

'Yesterday?'

'Yes.'

'Oh.'

That was all. She didn't even say anything about buying a new book or copying up, just 'Oh' – and then continued walking slowly up and down.

The next lesson was drama. At least there was no problem with books here, but Ollie felt uneasy. Burridge had left the classroom with a calculating glint in her eye.

'Right now, find a space and *relax*! Space, Jason, move away from Stephanie now. Space, James. Feel your spine dissolve, your bones melt, as you sink to the ground, down down down . . . now think of something pleasant while you lie there.'

All Ollie could think of was Burridge. What was she doing right now? In her mind's eye Ollie saw her, scrutinizing the letter from her mother, striding down the corridor. Any minute now she might enter the hall.

'I said *relax*, Ollie. You're like a balloon about to pop. Now everybody, when I say get up I want you to form groups and devise a situation in which one member has a secret, known to one other person, who betrays him or her to the rest of the group. Have you got that? I want to see what happens when the person is betrayed.'

Ollie's heart thudded against the floor. Did Miss Smart know too? Did everyone know? The others were on their feet looking for friends.

'Come on, Ollie.'

It was Hazel. Ollie searched her face. Had she . . .?

'Don't be crazy. It's just one of her ideas, or rather one of her *101 Ideas for Drama*. Haven't you seen her book? Look here's Melanie, pull yourself together or you'll give everything away. We've got to think of something.'

Secret meant only one thing to Ollie. She found it impossible to think of anything else. Fortunately Melanie had a brilliant idea, at least she thought it was a brilliant idea and since Hazel couldn't think of anything else either they acted it out.

At break Ollie was in deep gloom. The bogle had implied things would get better – *when* she had found it a home. She hadn't and they were getting worse. She was sure Burridge was going to confront her with her lie, and that she'd tell her father – it was just a matter of time. And she didn't know what to say. As usual Hazel thought she was worrying too much.

'Say they got soaked yesterday while walking from the bus to my house and then the dog got hold of them and finished them off.'

'She'll still get me for lying.'

'Tell her you didn't like to say so before because you didn't want to get me into trouble. I'll back you up if she asks.'

Ollie didn't like it. For a start all these lies were confusing her. But it would have to do, she didn't know what else to say. It didn't solve the money problem though and Burridge would be sure to make her pay for the lot. Trouble was she got a minute amount of pocket money a week. Hazel found some in her pocket and gave it to her.

'That and your pocket money should pay for two. How many were there?'

'Eight, I think. Mr Day has our RE books so that's one I haven't got to buy.'

'You can have my pocket money on Saturday. We might just do it. Have you any saved up?'

Ollie shook her head.

The bell rang for next lesson, social studies, medieval peasants again, but when Ollie was summoned to the front of the class her heart sank. A sixth former had just brought in a message from Miss Burridge. She was to go to her room at once.

'Well, Olwen?' Yellow fingers drummed a brown envelope. 'I'm waiting.' Burridge smelt of old ashtrays. She leaned back in her chair. 'I understand from Miss Quinn and Mr Sparrow that your English and science books are missing. I know that your maths and French books are missing. I assume that all your books are missing. Is that so?' Ollie nodded. 'I beg your pardon?'

'Yes.'

'Yes what?'

'Yes, Miss Burridge.'

'Well that's something. Perhaps now you will tell me truthfully what happened to them? I know that you did not cycle home last night, that the story you have hitherto told me is fictitious. A lie, Olwen.' As she said this she fingered a silver cross at her neck. 'I have been telling myself that there is some logical explanation. Well, perhaps we could hear it?'

'No.'

'Pardon?'

'No, Miss Burridge.'

'That is not what I meant!'

'I mean "No", there isn't a logical explanation.' It was the truth. Ollie was fed up with lies.

Burridge's mouth was open. Inside was like a tin-mine. At last she closed it and Ollie could see that she was thinking hard. And then she smiled. 'What would your father make of this, Olwen?'

So that was her game.

'I don't know.'

'And I don't suppose you would like him to know, would you? Would you?' She was still smiling. Ollie didn't answer. Burridge had the brown envelope in her hand. 'The bill, Olwen.' She handed it to her. 'You must do with it what you will. I – we simply require the cash – not a cheque, tomorrow please.'

Tomorrow! Ollie closed the door behind her. In the corridor she tore open the envelope. She couldn't possibly give it to her parents – and Burridge knew she couldn't. She unfolded the paper inside. TOTAL £7.65. £7.65! Impossible. Eight exercise books didn't cost that much. What was Burridge up to?

Chapter 11

'It's blackmail, Ollie. She knows you won't show it to your parents, so she's upped the bill to something ridiculous because she knows you can't argue – and it seems as if she doesn't care how you get the money.'

'And if I don't pay she'll tell my father!'

'There's only one thing to do – call her bluff.'

'What do you mean?'

'Tell your father. And the police. It's a crime, Ollie. You've got her!'

Ollie wasn't so sure. Burridge a criminal? It was scary. What if she did split and Burridge denied it? Called her a liar. She looked at the paper. It was plain, no school crest. Anybody could have written £7.65. Burridge would say Ollie had written it herself, and her father would probably believe her. And he would want to know how her books were destroyed and she couldn't tell him. She needed time to think. Where did the bogle come into this? Wouldn't it be better to find its home first? But if she made her father angry he would stop her from going to Hazel's.

Hazel's bus arrived. 'Think about it, Ol, I'll ring you.'

Ollie thought as she cycled home, taking yet another route, through Lampinscale village and then across the fields back to Lanthwaite. All the time she kept a lookout for eldertrees. If she could find one before the weekend then surely the bogle would be placated and stop tormenting her. There were none – and it took her ages to get home pushing her bike along overgrown paths and cattle grids, lifting it over stiles. She was late and her mum was tearful.

'I've been worried about you, Ollie love, it's half past five.'

Mr Hindmarch came in, still angry about the stolen peregrine eggs, said it proved they would have to be even more vigilant next spring. The only good thing was that the committee would be prepared, were all determined that the nest on Ghyll Crag would be guarded twenty-four hours day and night. Miss Burridge, the new secretary, had said she would organize the rota. After the meal he went to the phone to arrange the next meeting. Ollie felt ill.

She went upstairs. Listened. Tried to hear what he was saying. Waited for him to come off the phone. But when he did, he didn't yell for her, or come rushing upstairs. So Burridge couldn't have told him yet. She must be waiting for the cash.

Ollie searched her room and found a book token for £1. Her head ached, there was so much to think about. It was true that one lie led to another, led perhaps to other things as well. She had begun to think of where she might find money around the house. The only place she could think of was the egg-money jar. Her mother sold the eggs they couldn't eat and kept the money on the window-sill. Her dad was always telling her not to, it was too handy for thieves. Thieves! No! She wasn't a thief. What was the bogle doing to her?

She tried to do her homework, but all she could think of was the money. She couldn't take the egg fund. It was wrong and it was risky. When they discovered it was missing they'd be sure to blame her. She would have to find it some other way. Hazel – it was obvious the Jehus were rich – she would borrow it from her.

Downstairs the phone rang. That was probably her now. It was and she'd managed to get a month's pocket money in advance. That left only £1.05 to find. Where? Were there some beer bottles at the bottom of the garden with money back on return? She wished she'd looked when it was light. It was nine o'clock and dark. Time for bed in fact.

Later, after her mother had said goodnight and put out the light, Ollie lay in bed thoughts whirring. Find the money find the tree, find the money find the tree. Where was the bogle anyway? Was it only last night it had been in her room scattering paper? She lay awake listening. The clock ticked. Did something tap at the window? Yes. No. If it did she wouldn't ignore it this time. She would get up. Something creaked. She reached out her arm and put on her bedside lamp, looked around, got out of bed, looked under the bed, tiptoed to the window. It was hard to see out with the polythene there, but she stood for several minutes and listened. Put her face close to the polythene and tried to see out. There was nothing. She crept back to the bed and put out the lamp to see better outside, felt her way back to the window. There was still nothing just the dark starless night. Nothing out there that wanted to come in, she was sure, and she did want to be sure.

In bed again she whispered to the darkness – just in case, 'I've found a tree, well, Hazel has. Wait till Friday. I'll take you.' Listened. Thought she heard a snigger. Find the money find the money find the money . . . she felt as if she had a record in her head, spinning at too great a speed . . . findthemoneyfindthemoneyfindthe money . . .

'Stop. Calm down.' She was talking to herself but it was the only way to stop the jabbering inside her head. She dredged her mind for ideas. £1.05 wasn't a vast sum. You could get more than that for writing a letter to a magazine or doing a paper round – but not by tomorrow morning. Did she have to? Yes, or else Burridge would tell her father, he would stop her going to Hazel's, and then she'd never find a home for the bogle.

Eventually she fell asleep but spent a restless night. In her dreams eldertrees galloped about the countryside, branches twisting, roots twitching. Stoats, mice and hedgehogs fled from their grasp.

'No! No!'

'Ollie!'

They'd caught her.

'Ollie, wake up.'

'No! No . . . Oh, hello, Mum.'

She was shaking her arm.

'What were you doing? Now wake up and get dressed. We're late. It's gone eight o'clock.'

Downstairs, her dad was just leaving for work.

'Late, aren't you? Better get a move on. And mind your Ps and Qs at school today. I'll be seeing your Miss Burridge tonight.'

Tonight! If only he hadn't said that. She was eating cornflakes at the time but her throat closed instantly. Coughing she staggered to the sink, spat, and then got herself a drink of water. The egg money was in the jar on the window-sill – in front of her. Tonight, he'd said. Then she must find the money – now. Her hand nearly got stuck as she drew the coins out, and she crept out of the door like a criminal.

Chapter 12

Instantly she regretted it. She didn't even know how much she'd taken. Ought to stop and see but her legs kept pushing the pedals, propelling her forward as if she were being chased. Several times she glanced over her shoulder, expected to see her father, or a police car with its siren blaring. All she could hear was the intake of her own breath, and the road behind her was empty; she had taken the back route which was nearly always deserted.

She hadn't meant to take the money. She'd decided the night before that it was a bad idea. It was wrong. It would create more problems than it would solve. Then why had she done it? It was as if her hand had carried out some previously arranged plan, hadn't received the message that the plan had been cancelled. Perhaps that's why they chopped the hands off thieves in some countries. Cruel. It was the hand's fault, not hers; she wasn't a thief. She wasn't. She would put back the money just as soon as she could.

The road was steeper now and her legs were tired. She was panting. Would have to stop and push the bike to the top of the hill. On the left was a field with ponies on the far side. She leaned her bike against the gate and took the money from her pocket – three pound coins and 36p in change. How much did she need? Only £1.05. She fumbled in her bag for the envelope. It was while she was trying to work out what to do, first what to give Miss Burridge, and then how to put the rest of it back – after all her mother might not know how much there was, she could put the rest back later – when she felt the hand on her shoulder.

She stiffened. Dread filled her. So soon. Was the game up so soon? She felt hot breath on her neck, felt her knees go rubbery as if her legs would give way. Who was it? Father? Police? She waited for someone to speak. Waited, felt a tickling sensation on the back of her neck which made her want to move away. Couldn't move. Felt sick. Wanted to scream, 'Speak will you! Whoever you are, speak. Say something!' But she couldn't even mouth the words. Her mouth was dry. The tightness in her throat hurt. She wanted to cry and yet at the same time there was the tickling which made her want to laugh.

'Hrrrrmph!'

'Aaaagh!' She screamed.

'Hrrrrmph!'

More hot breath on her neck – and spray too. And the sound? Hardly human. She turned round half knowing. Laughed with relief. A pony! A black Shetland pony with a long fringe over its eyes. That's what she had felt, resting its muzzle on her shoulder, tickling her with its whiskers. Two others were ambling towards the gate, one brown and white, one brown. There wasn't time to pat them. She must sort out the money which was cutting into her hand. Next, get to school, find Hazel, get the £5, give it to Burridge, hope she would accept the book token as part of the bill.

That bit was easy. Hardly looking at her, Burridge took the money and the token and, Ollie noted, she put it all in her own bag.

All day Ollie thought about the stolen money. Would her mother have discovered the theft? Would she have told her father? Would it be possible to explain and put some money back and promise the rest later? She cycled home by the main road, the quickest route. There was no point in looking for eldertrees, she had scoured the area and there were none, and there was no point in delaying her return. Better to get home before her father and try to put things right.

But as soon as she saw the house she knew she was doomed. There was her father's car in the drive. She got off her bike, wanted to turn round and cycle away again, anywhere, just as long as she didn't have to be accused of stealing. The boys next door were coming out of their drive now, arms spread, making an ear-shattering roaring sound.

'Mind out! Mind out! You're on the runway!'

She moved to one side. And there was her father coming out of the garage. He didn't see her, went round the back of the house.

'Mind out! Mind out!'

They were coming back. She couldn't move any further to the side without being in the hedge. They swerved past her. Where could she go? She wanted to shrink, hide beneath the hedge. She couldn't. It was no good, she would have to go in, hope for the best. She trudged up the drive, put her bike in the garage and opened the kitchen door.

Her mother and father were sitting at the table, a pot of tea between them. When Ollie entered they didn't say anything, though she had the feeling they had been saying something just a moment before. She didn't say anything either. She wanted to but even something as ordinary as 'hello' seemed out of place. She stood there for a moment and then went into the hall to take off her coat. Something was up, there was no doubt about that. Should she go upstairs or back into the kitchen?

'Ollie.' Her mother's voice. 'Ollie.' Well, that settled it, she supposed. Back in the kitchen Mrs Hindmarch was pouring more water into the pot.

'Sit down, Ollie love.' Ollie sat, her mother one side, father the other.

'Like a cup of tea, dear?'

'Please.' She poured it out and handed it to Ollie.

'What sort of day have you had, dear?'

'All right. Boring.'

'Oh dear, Ollie love, you always say that.'

There was a splutter then *bang* went her father's mug on the table, splashing tea over the cloth. 'All right, where is it?'

Ollie watched the khaki stain spread.

'Where is it?' He thrust his red face against hers.

'What?' She looked him straight in the eye.

'You know what!'

'I don't. I don't know what you're talking about.'

Afterwards – in her room of course – she wondered how she had had the nerve.

He had shouted, banged the table with his fist, stood up, towered over her, looked as if he was going to hit her and she had just sat there saying, 'I don't know what you mean.' This had enraged him further. He strode over to the window-sill, grabbed the empty jar and slammed it down before her.

'This! Your're not telling me you don't know anything about this?'

'Yes.'

'Ah!'

'I mean no.'

There followed one of those awkward yes-no confusions with his thinking she had confessed and her being quite sure she hadn't. Or had she? Denying knowledge of the jar was silly, near to admitting there was something to deny. Better to have said, 'It's the egg-money jar' or something like that, but it was difficult to think.

Her mother cried and tried to clear the table. Mr Hindmarch told her to get out of the way and sat down again.

'Look at me, Ollie. Now, are you telling me that you haven't stolen the money from this jar?'

Ollie thought carefully. The way he phrased his questions made them difficult to answer. 'Yes' sounded like a confession but was the right answer – the right wrong answer that is. It was all so difficult. For a moment she considered telling the truth – the 'whole truth and nothing but the truth' as they said in films – but dismissed it.

'Yes,' she answered.

'You didn't steal the money?'

'No.' She hadn't stolen it, just borrowed. She was going to put it back. If only he was the sort of person you could talk to. If only she could say, 'Well there was this elder bogle who's angry because you've chopped down its home, and it tore up all my books because I haven't found it a new one yet, and your Miss Burridge says we've got to pay for new ones and she's doubled the price . . .' Well, she could imagine how that would go down.

'Take that smirk off your face!'

She'd known what was coming next.

'And get up to your room!' She stood up. 'And this time, Olwen, you can stay there. No weekending with posh friends. I'm determined to get to the bottom of this and you can stay there till I do.'

She went upstairs and stayed there till late that night. Only when she was sure her parents were asleep did she creep downstairs. She would put the money back.

All but a pound of it anyway. She would return that when she got it. It wasn't a perfect solution but it would make her feel better, and it might change her father's mind about the weekend.

It was dark and cold in the kitchen. She didn't dare put the light on, felt her way forward, groped in the darkness for furniture and familiar landmarks – table, sink unit, and behind it the window-sill. Would the jam-jar be there? The rubbery leaves of a potted plant touched her hand, a clammy dish-cloth. Glass. That must be it. She had the money in her right hand. With her left she took the jar down, went to slide the money inside, but what was that? Something there already. Odd. No not odd, her mother could have sold some eggs. But she hadn't heard anyone come to the door. Perhaps it wasn't money at all. Carefully, so as not to make a noise, she put the cash she was holding on the draining board and drew out the contents of the jar. It was money. £3.36. Exactly the amount she had taken. Odd. She could see because it had become lighter. She looked outside expecting to see the moon but there was none, and then she heard the sound of water rushing. There was someone in the bathroom upstairs! That was what the light was. The bathroom was directly above the kitchen.

She froze. Prayed that no one would look into her bedroom or worse, come downstairs for a drink. The cooker clock whirred loudly. She jumped as the fridge throbbed into action. Then it went dark upstairs and she heard footsteps. Creak. Creak. Creak. They stopped. A long creak next. Somebody getting into bed she thought, but carried on listening. She must wait before going back upstairs in case someone was still awake, and she must decide what to do about the money. It was very odd. As if it hadn't been taken at all. Very odd. What should she do? She still didn't want the money. It made her feel dirty somehow keeping it. She would put it back, but first she must find it. It was on the draining board somewhere. She felt the cold surface. Ah there it was. She put the money in the jar, placed the jar on the window-sill, and crept back to bed.

Chapter 13

When she woke up she didn't go downstairs. She was still confused by the night's events. What would her parents do now? She didn't have to wait long to see. There was a knock on the door and her mother came in.

'It's all right, Ollie love, there's been a mistake. My fault, dear, I hadn't looked properly. There were two jars on the window-sill and I only saw the empty one. The egg-money jar was behind the curtain. Silly me I know, and I'm sorry for all the trouble I've caused. I've explained to your dad and he's not at all pleased with me.'

Ollie could imagine.

'He's pleased of course that it wasn't you, Ollie. I told him he was very wrong to think you'd do a thing like that. Come on now you'd better get up and get your things together.'

Ollie kept her face hidden. She couldn't be sure what expression it would show. She had taken the money and her mother was saying she hadn't.

'In fact, Ollie, it's all turned out very well, there was even more in the jar than I remembered. I found it this morning. Come on now. You've got to get your things ready for the weekend too, you're going to the Jehus, aren't you? I didn't get time to tell you yesterday but Dr Jehu rang up and said she would pick you up from school and put your bike in the back of the car. You'll only need your nightie and some jeans and a jumper, won't you – and a toothbrush and spare pants. You won't need a case, you couldn't carry one on your bike anyhow. Your dad's already gone to work by the way. He was on early shift.'

Downstairs Ollie found it hard to speak, didn't know what to say. It was too good to be true. What was her mum up to? Twice she said, 'You wouldn't do a thing like that, would you?' and each time Ollie shook her head. It was while going out of the door that the biggest surprise came. Bending to kiss her, her mum thrust something into her hand, a pound coin.

She raced to school, optimistic now. Things were going well. Tonight she would find the new eldertree. The bogle would have its winter home. There would be no more disasters. Only one thing niggled her. 'Yan tyan tethera,' it had said – three tasks. What was the third?

Four o'clock came at last. When she told Hazel about the money, Hazel said her mum seemed real nice. She obviously knew Ollie had taken it but was giving her a chance to put things right. She thought Ollie ought to tell her the truth – in confidence. Ollie wasn't so sure – about anything. It was odd, her mum was usually so short of money she didn't see how she could have found more so quickly.

'Well, how do you think the money got back in the jar?'

Ollie didn't answer.

'How . . . oh, Ollie, not the bogle?' She shook her head. 'No. No. It couldn't have. Well I hope not, because if it did, it would have to have got the money from somewhere and that could mean more trouble . . . no, I'm sure it was your mother. Look, here's mine!'

Dr Jehu's station wagon was drawing up to the kerb.

'Pile in, girls.' She opened the doors and they hoisted Ollie's bike into the back of the car, then piled in and set off.

Ollie hoped the bogle was in her bag – or somewhere about. She hadn't seen it since Tuesday. After showering her room with paper it had disappeared. Where did it go when it wasn't tormenting her? Could it shrink? Become invisible? She looked up at the sky. Blue. Cloudless. No sign of rain this time. As soon as they got to Scawthwaite they must find the tree, hope the bogle would like it.

They went outside as soon as they got home, didn't stop to change out of their uniforms, ran to the village. Seeing the tree, Ollie felt sure it was exactly what the bogle had demanded. The top was bushy and still green-leaved. The twisted trunk was split up one side, dark within. It was heavy with glistening black berries. Only one thing worried her. It was too near people, in the middle of a farmyard in fact.

'Ollie! Quit worrying. It's got to like it. It's the only eldertree for miles. We've proved that.'

It was true.

'Look, leave your bag there, under the tree – with the zip open – that's all we can do really.'

It was and it was very unsatisfactory. They watched from a nearby pigsty, their backs against the gate and Hazel was if anything even more curious than Ollie, and wouldn't keep quiet.

'Ollie, how big did you say it was?'

'I didn't.'

'But how big is it?'

'I don't know, it varies.'

'But . . .'

'Look, Hazel, let's either go away and talk about it or stay here and be quiet.'

But Ollie didn't want to go away. She wanted to wait. Wanted to see the bogle make one of its lightning leaps – from her bag to the tree. Only then would she be sure. She glanced at her watch. Nearly five.

'Ollie . . .'

'Shh.'

The sun was low in the sky, would soon sink behind Skiddle. Several cats appeared, thin hungry creatures, meal on their whiskers. A rat hung from the jaws of a ginger. A grey slunk by with a vole. Was the bogle watching them too? Is that why it didn't appear? When Mr Pattinson roared into the yard on his tractor the cats scattered. A one-eyed tabby shot into the eldertree, hid in its branches. Was that its one eye glinting, caught by a last ray of sun, or was it . . .? She couldn't be sure.

Still they waited. Skiddle was black now against a pink and gold sky. Mr Pattinson, a short dark man with enormous eyebrows, said: 'How do?' Hazel said, 'How do?' back. Ollie kept her eyes on the tree. The farmer went into the house. Still they waited, till looking at her watch, Hazel said they ought to be going home. Dinner would be ready. Ollie said yes but didn't move.

'We can leave the bag, Ollie, and come back after.'

So they did, Ollie walking backwards till she could no longer see the tree.

When they got back it was beginning to grow dark. There was a pale moon and their shadows preceded them like long thin giants. Hens roosted on the straw stack and settled grunts came from the sties. Cats watched from shed roofs. A mouse scuttled from stack to sty. Three cats sprang, gave chase, but the mouse ran under the door.

Their backs against the sty, Ollie and Hazel watched

the tree, just a black shape now. They heard the leaves rustle, wondered, watched the bag. The evening star appeared. It was quite cold. Ollie wondered how she would know when the bogle was settled in the tree if she didn't in fact see it enter. Was it there already? She supposed, hoped, things would start getting better, that the series of things going wrong would come to an end, but what she longed for was a sign.

She looked at her watch again, thought she felt rain. More bad luck. It wouldn't do to leave her bag out all night and have it ruined. She felt low. She'd wanted so much more than this. If only she could have been sure that it had been in the bag. Why couldn't it show itself when she wanted it to? She looked up. There were several stars in the sky.

Even Hazel was glum. 'I'm sorry, Ol, we'll have to go. My folks'll get jittery if we're not home soon.'

Trees and buildings were just outlines now and it was definitely raining, a fine persistent drizzle, which felt as if it had set in for the night. Reluctantly she agreed, they'd better get back, come again tomorrow.

'I'll get the bag.' Feeling heavy inside she approached the tree.

The bag was in fact dry, sheltered by the branches. She bent down to pick it up, and at the time it didn't seem odd when rain stung her cheek. Hardly noticing, she wiped it with her hand and walked back to Hazel who was standing by the gate with a torch. Dazzling her eyes with it she was, and looking gormless.

'Stop that, Hazel. I can't see!'

'Ollie!'

'What?'

'Ollie!'

'WHAT?'

She was grinning stupidly and heavens, were those tears in her eyes?

'Purple rain, Ollie, running down your cheek. Purple! A sign Ollie, a sign!'

Ollie looked down at her fingers. They were smeared with purple juice.

Chapter 14

They raced home, not because of the rain. They couldn't have cared less about the rain. They ran because they couldn't stop themselves. They shouted too and laughed and hugged each other like footballers who had just scored the winning goal. Two old men on their way to the pub stared at them, but this just made them laugh more. When they reached the open road which led to Hazel's house they were exhausted, had to stop for a while to gather their breath.

'Well?'

'Well?'

There wasn't a lot to say really. Words couldn't express the marvellous feeling of freedom Ollie had, which Hazel seemed to share. They ran again, all the way to the house.

It was a wonderful weekend. Ollie couldn't remember ever enjoying herself so much – and it was more important than she realized at the time. On the Saturday they went to the stone circle – they being Ollie, Hazel, Hazel's dad and the dog. Ollie knew the way; she had been there many times before with her father on Peregrine Watch.

'You have to leave the car here, Mr Jehu.'

'Thank you, Miss Hindmarch.'

'Sorry.'

They were in a small car park, just a clearing between

some trees really, on the edge of the woods. There was already one car there, a blue Ford Escort. Instinctively Ollie noted the number to check it against her father's list of suspicious ones when she got home. She didn't need to write it down.

'Hazel, look.'

'Hey, Peter, look.'

All three goggled at the number plate. Mr Jehu got his camera out of the car.

'Stand by it, Ollie. Pity it isn't a Rolls-Royce.'

The registration read OLL218Y.

It was a long, upward trek to the stone circle, spiralling the fell, first through woodland, lacy with larch, and then through knee-high bracken and golden bilberry bushes. Higher up was slippery sheep-cropped grass, and streams springing, trickling, vanishing underground. Looking up all they could see was the rising fell, russet, then grey-green, mottled beneath passing clouds. Then, rounding a headland they saw them against a sheet of blue sky, the ring of stones, commanding attention as they had for thousands of years.

Daunted, they paused, then turned and surveyed the scene behind them. Miles away lay Sleadle Water like a gigantic mirror, reflecting forest, mountains and silky clouds.

Mr Jehu was impressed. 'Stone Age man must have liked walking – or had a very good reason for building up here. I hope he didn't have to carry those rocks.'

They were facing uphill again when they noticed two figures ahead, carrying climbing gear. Ollie had the feeling that she knew one of them. Silly really, you can't tell much from a back view; she couldn't even be sure what sex the one on the left was, wearing a track suit and a woolly hat. The other one was bearded. She must ask about the car. The two must be intending to abseil down the side of Ghyll Crag. It wasn't forbidden at this time of year, they couldn't harm nests or anything, but any strangers on the crag had to be noted, especially if they had climbing equipment. They could be practising for a later raid.

They'd stopped now, were looking behind them, the hatted one through binoculars. Why hadn't she thought of that?

'Mr . . . Peter, may I borrow your glasses?'

'Of course, Ollie.' He handed them to her, but it was too late. By the time she had focused them, they'd turned away and were walking down the fell instead.

'Well they won't do much climbing down there,' said Mr Jehu consulting his map. 'That path only leads to Rake Foot Farm.' Ollie trained the glasses on the disappearing profile of the hatted one, thought but didn't say anything, that it looked like Miss Burridge.

When they passed the turning the two strangers were already out of sight. Ahead was a fence, a stile over it. Beyond, at the far side of the field, near the edge of the headland, was the ring of stones.

Mr Jehu leaned on the stile. For several seconds no one spoke.

'There's definitely something about the place, isn't there, girls?'

There was. Ollie had felt it before.

They were near to the place where the peregrine watchers had their tent in the spring but she didn't mention this, wished she'd never mentioned it. She hoped Mr Jehu wouldn't ask. Her father said she mustn't tell anyone.

They climbed over the stile, walked silently to the centre of the circle. Even the dog seemed impressed by the something and was quiet and still. Ollie counted forty-nine stones, some of them house high, some almost buried. Absorbed, and not noticing the others walk away, she turned round, gazed beyond the stones to the surrounding mountains, beyond them to the encircling sky. Circle within circle within circle, she was the hub of a triple circle. She shivered.

'Ollie!' Hazel was standing by the tallest stone with Cerberus straining at the leash. There were sheep in a neighbouring field. 'Come on. I'm walking round three times and wishing!'

'What for?'

'What you like. Come on!'

It was silly and at the same time it wasn't. And it seemed greedy to wish; she had never been so happy in her life; all her wishes recently had been granted. She thought hard. Was there anything else she wanted?

'Come on! Cerby and I have started.'

Yes, so she ran to the outside of the circle and began to stump from stone to stone very deliberately, staring at her feet, repeating her wish. Mr Jehu took photographs.

Hazel was ahead of her. When she gave a shout Ollie strode on, though she saw through the corner of her eye walkers approaching, cameras, maps and glasses swinging from their necks. Hazel had turned round.

'We'd better stop; they'll think we're crazy.'

But Ollie shook her head. She didn't want to stop. She had to keep going, had to complete the three circuits. Yan tyan tethera. Hazel started off again. The tourists were talking to Mr Jehu now. Ollie heard 'Gee thanks', heard the clicks of cameras but still kept walking. Only when the whole group came closer and then began to tramp after her, did the urge to run away fight the urge to continue. But hot-faced, she carried on. Hazel too continued till she reached the tallest stone for the third time, when she ran to Peter and started pummelling his chest.

'What did you say to them, Peter? I've never been so embarrassed in my life!' Mr Jehu was laughing and trying to protect himself.

'Oh, not a lot. They asked what you were doing and I said it was an ancient druid custom to walk round the circle three times and wish, and obviously they decided to walk round the circle three times and wish. What are you hitting me for? It was your idea.'

'It was a joke.'

'OK. It was a joke.'

'But they believed you.'

'So?'

'It was a lie.'

'Oh, that's a bit harsh. Poetic licence I would call it.'

Ollie couldn't understand them. Poetic licence? What did he mean?

'He means it's all right to tell lies if it makes a good story.'

All right to tell lies? She was more confused than ever.

Shouts of 'Have a nice day' interrupted them. Their three circuits completed, the five Americans waved and set off across the field.

'And I hope their wishes come true – and yours,' said Mr Jehu. 'Now where was this peregrine nest that your father cares so much about?'

Ollie felt herself blushing. How could she answer without being rude? When he had been so kind? Besides if he went to the far edge of the circle, he could see it – where it had been that is.

'I'm sorry but I'm not allowed to tell anyone. Er . . . Peter.' She added that so as to sound less rude, but it sounded even ruder.

'Oh, Ollie, you can tell Peter, he . . .'

Her father was shaking his head. 'It's all right, Ollie, I understand. You don't know me very well, and if these magnificent birds are to survive in the wild they have to be guarded with the utmost secrecy. It's good they have people like you and your father to protect them. Here, have some fudge.'

They sat down on the grass and ate it.

'We'll go to a pub for lunch, shall we?'

They were getting to their feet when a sharp cry high above made the three of them look up.

Kek. Kek. Silver flashed against the blue sky as beating wings caught the sun. Swooped then rose again, swooped again. The peregrine. Suddenly it stopped. Wings flexed, it dive-bombed something below. A white shape fell from the sky; white feathers floated down. Above, silver turned to slate, slate to silver. Arched wings still now, the peregrine pursued its prey. More silver wing beats. More. Past them it soared now. Over the precipice. Gone.

Awed, they stood for several moments, then they walked to the side of the crag and looked down. Far far below, all they could see was a shower of feathers, the falcon stripping its prey. Ollie was glad she wasn't closer, shook her head when Mr Jehu offered field glasses.

None of them spoke much as they made their way down, not even Mr Jehu, so Hazel's whisper made Ollie jump. They were about to climb over the stile. She looked in the direction of Hazel's pointed finger, saw a tree further along the wall. There were several in fact round the edge of the field. What was so special about this one?

'Look at that one. Hard.'

Ollie looked.

It was an eldertree heavy with berries. Yan tyan tethera. She didn't know why she thought that, but she did.

When they reached the car park theirs was the only car. OLL218Y had gone.

Chapter 15

That wonderful day was the last of summer. Squally weather followed, and one day as she pushed her bike down the drive, Ollie noticed a single leaf clinging to the topmost branch of the apple tree. The next day it had gone. Soon, snow shawled the highest fells and then the low ones. Streams froze. Icicles like giants' fingers hung where mountain streams had fallen. Mr Hindmarch took long lonely walks. This was how he liked it, no trippers littering the countryside, no guests filling his house. Not that it made him any happier. He was as grumpy as ever. Mrs Hindmarch said he had money problems. That was the trouble when they had no visitors – no money either. He was impatient for spring too. Miss Burridge, 'efficient woman', had already worked out the rota for a twenty-four hour a day Peregrine Watch.

For Ollie the excruciating boredom of school was relieved by having Hazel as a friend. She was clever so teachers liked her and they seemed to like Ollie better too. Melanie and Tracy of course liked her less. Burridge was very odd, took to calling her 'Olwen dear' and found her jobs to do in breaks and dinner hours. She had become very friendly with Mr Hindmarch. Mentioned him quite frequently. It was nauseating.

From time to time Ollie wondered about the bogle. Her life was better. Not perfect but better. Was it hibernating? Was its tree all right? More worrying, had it got a third task for her to do? Hazel hadn't seen it, but then Hazel never had. As the weeks passed by she reported that the tree was bare or covered with snow, and one day in April she said that the first leaves had appeared. Hearing this, Ollie went down to the bottom of the garden. The stump was a crown of green shoots!

It was in late April that Mr Hindmarch came home with what passed for a smile on his face. The peregrines had laid. There were two eggs in the nest. Two men from the Mountain Rescue team had checked and the watch had already begun. His rota was working like clockwork. He'd be doing Saturday nights himself – with Miss Burridge.

Ollie couldn't believe it. Last year she'd shared the watch with him, wanted to this year.

'That was during the day, lass. Besides, this year we're not having children up there. The committee have decided it's too dangerous. And kids talk.'

'But, Dad . . .'

'No buts. Sorry, Olwen. Cynthia and I have got it all worked out. There'll be no mistakes this year.'

Cynthia! Ollie thought she would explode. Instead she went to bed. She exploded to Hazel in the morning.

To cheer her up, Hazel invited her for the weekend. It turned out to be the most exciting weekend of her life, though it began ordinarily enough. On the Saturday, they played records, watched television, walked around the village and visited Pattinson's Farm twice. They saw nothing unusual. The leaves of the eldertree were a fresh new green. There was no sign from the bogle.

It was very late, after they had gone to bed, that things began to happen. First, Ollie was surprised to find herself awake, sitting upright in bed and wondering why. She looked, but couldn't see Hazel who was asleep in the other bed, when suddenly the room was filled with light. Dark again. A noise like a train rattled the windowpanes. Hazel's voice: 'What was that?'

'You awake?'

'No, I'm asleep.'

'Sorry. Thunder, I think.'

'Switch on the light; it's nearest you.'

Ollie felt for the lamp and pressed the switch. Nothing happened.

'It must be off at the wall; it doesn't work.'

'Hold on, I'll try the switch by the door.'

Ollie saw Hazel's shadow move past the end of the bed, heard a click but no light came on.

'Must be a power cut.'

Ollie remembered the last 'power cut'.

There was another flash of lightning. She counted. One . . . two . . . crrrRR . . . ASH!

'It's very near.'

They both made their way to the window and looked out, pressed their faces to the glass but could see nothing. Outside, wind howled and rain drummed on the garage roof. Another flash of lightning made them step back. More thunder. For a second they could see the church tower in Scawthwaite and a single Scots pine. Dark again and the rain beat down.

Hazel yawned. 'No point in staying here. We'd be better off in b – '

Zigzag lightning cut her off mid-sentence. An enormous cracking sound shook the house. They clung together. For a few seconds it was dark, then, as they watched the village, a ribbon of orange flame unfurled itself, and like a giant firework exploded.

Ollie knew instantly what it was. Tethera! The elder-tree had been struck by lightning.

'I've got to go!' She nearly knocked Hazel over.

'Are you crazy?'

'Probably, but I've got to go.' She was already scrabbling under the bed for shoes.

'Waterproofs. Where are they? If you don't know, leave it. I'll go without.'

'Stop panicking, Ollie. I'll get Helen, she'll take us there in the car.'

As Ollie pulled on she-didn't-know-what clothes she heard the bedroom door go. A few minutes later Hazel was back.

'Mum's not there and Dad's away. I expect she's been called out on an emergency. There'll be a note somewhere but I can't see it. I found these in Dad's wardrobe.'

They were jackets of some kind.

They let themselves out of the front door and fought their way through the rain to the village. By this time there was a huge bonfire ahead. Flames leapt above the house-tops and raindrops glittered as they caught the light. Entering the village they heard voices.

'Pattinson's Farm.'

'Tree it was. Caught by lightning.'

Ollie knew it.

Hazel was her practical self. 'It's very near that straw stack. I hope someone's phoned the fire brigade. We should have.'

'Someone has, lass, but it'll be half an hour 'fore it gits here.'

The farm buildings were clearly visible. Mr Pattinson, holding a hose, was directing water over the eldertree. Other people had buckets but couldn't reach the flames. Several rushed about with soaking sacks, hanging them over the straw stack. The tree was an enormous flame-torch, the trunk white, the branches streams of fire.

'Exploded it did. You should have seen it. Shot the bark right off. Whoosh!'

The man demonstrated, throwing his arms out wide.

The bogle. Where was it? The ground was covered with shattered bark.

'We've got to find it, Hazel. Got to.'

They crouched on the wet ground and searched where they could. Picked up scraps of bark and examined them. Hazel brought pieces to Ollie. She wasn't exactly sure what they were looking for, as she still hadn't seen the bogle. They found nothing. Ollie feared the worst. Were the charred fragments at their feet simply eldertree or were they pieces of the sprite? How could they examine all of them? Near the fire it was too dangerous. A short distance away it was too dark. A single torch beam made searching slow work. It also meant getting in people's way, being shouted at. Absorbed they didn't hear a siren bleating.

'Stand back! Stand back!'

'In that sty, lass. You'll be safe there.'

The fire engine at last. It roared into the yard, firemen leaping in all directions. Within minutes water cascaded from massive hoses and the fire was out.

Now what? The girls looked around them. The sty was empty; the pigs had obviously been moved somewhere else in case the fire spread. Some folk were going into the farmhouse, most were wandering home, talking as they went.

'Lucky, very lucky they were, just that ol' tree.'

'Elder a bloody nuisance anyhow.'

Just that old tree. Ollie wanted to cry. Hazel already was.

'Don't, Hazel. I can't bear it.'

'What? Don't what?'

'Cry.'

'I'm not.'

But there it was again, a sob, a whimpering sound.

'Isn't that you?'

'No. I thought it was you.'

They both had the thought at the same time. Could it be? They listened again. Sob.

It was coming from the ground. On hands and knees they strained their eyes to see by the light that came from the farmhouse. And then they saw it, in the corner, a crumpled quivering creature, charred, with no strength to move. Ollie crawled over, picked it up and gently cradled it in her hands.

'All right bogle, all right. There there.'

Hazel stepped out of the darkness, dropped to her knees. It was some seconds before she spoke.

'It's beautiful, Ollie. You didn't say it was beautiful.'

'Yes. Sometimes, but quiet, Hazel, it's saying something. Listen.'

'It's crying.'

'No it isn't. Listen.'

'Sap. Sap.'

Sap not sob! Yes, she remembered, it had to have sap. But where? Where? Where had they seen another eldertree? Of course. She stood up. 'We've got to move! Quickly.'

'Yes, I know, the stone circle!'

But how to get there quickly?

There were two old bikes leaning on the farmhouse wall outside. Most people were inside the house. The firemen rolling up the hoses wouldn't know the bikes weren't theirs.

'We'll borrow them – it's an emergency.'

It was. The bogle, silent now, lay lifeless in her hands.

'Hang on, don't die. I'm taking you to a new home. New home,' she repeated, slipping it into the large pocket of Mr Jehu's jacket. 'New home.'

Chapter 16

There was no short cut. They had to go three miles into Helmswick, and then out on the Whinrith road to the stone circle – another mile or so. Then they would have to walk. No taking bikes up that slope. It was a clear night with a threequarter moon – the storm had cleared the clouds away – and they could avoid bumps and holes in the road. Ollie, fearing for the bogle's life, tried not to knock it. The worst things were the cattle grids. Three times they had to get off their bikes and lift them over, careful not to squash the pocket in which the bogle rested.

Helmswick was dead. The church clock struck twelve as they entered the town. A cat was crossing the empty market place, but there was no time to think of the witching hour or anything else. All they must do was pedal furiously, and keep a lookout. They didn't want police asking what they were doing. Twice cars passed them but none of them stopped. Perhaps they didn't look like girls with their rain-soaked hair, men's jackets and ancient bikes. Ollie hoped not.

It seemed an age before they came to the turning to the car park. Woods lined the roads here. It was much, much spookier. Easy to see figures moving among the trees, watching them. Noises too – long sighs and the crunch of footsteps. But it was a time to keep imagination in check. At last, the car park – and two cars in it. Two she recognized – one was her father's old Vauxhall, the other OLL218Y! Very odd, she'd mentioned it to her father and he'd written it down. It wasn't one of the suspected ones, but it wasn't a local one either. She hadn't bothered to say she'd thought Miss Burridge was in it. No mystery about her father's car. It was Saturday night and he must be above the crag watching – with Cynthia!

Ollie felt sick but this was no time to feel sorry for herself. Something made her want to hide the bikes. No point in letting her father know they were there and, though they should be away before the night watch finished at six, you never knew. They pushed them underneath the wire that bordered the car park and then behind some trees. Ollie pulled up some moss to make a soft bed for the bogle.

'How is it?'

'I don't know. Very still.' She lifted it out for Hazel to hold while she lined her pocket with moss.

'It's very dry. Quite badly burnt.'

'Slip it in here now, the moss is damp. I thought it might help.'

They climbed the slope as fast as they could, but kept sliding over the wet grass into streams, and mud clung to their feet sucking them down. Ollie worried, first about the bogle, secondly about her father and Miss Burridge. She and Hazel didn't talk. If they were discovered after they'd returned the bogle to the elder-tree, too bad – trouble, but she was used to that. If they were seen before they managed to return it, then she didn't know what would happen.

The moon washed everything with brilliant light. It was really odd that they hadn't been seen. Odd too about the car parked beside her father's. Climbers, the owners had been. They'd carried ropes. It was fishy.

Did her dad know it was there? If she hadn't had the bogle to worry about she'd have gone up and told him.

Ghost-sheep munched silently. When did they sleep? On a far fell a fox coughed. Unaware the sheep munched on. The girls walked as fast as they could, the ancient stones now visible above them. Did eyes watch them? Did danger lurk? It would be so easy to hide behind a boulder or simply lie flat on the ground. Wet though. Not far now. They could see the wall and the stile which led to the stone circle. And there was the tree about twenty metres along.

Almost there, but the bogle in her pocket hadn't moved.

'What's that?' Hazel had stopped and was whispering. Ollie stopped too, but all she could hear was running water.

'I can't h – '

'Ssh. Listen. There it is again.'

This time Ollie heard it, a groaning. It was coming from higher up the path.

There it was again. A moaning, groaning sound. What?

'Quick Ollie! Someone's hurt!'

It could be a trick. Ollie stayed still and looked round, but Hazel was scrambling up the slope as fast as she could. Ollie couldn't let her go alone. The groans were louder now and soon they could make out a shape on the path ahead of them.

'H – elp. Help!'

'Hold on. We're coming.'

Part of Ollie still wanted Hazel to shut up, at least stop a moment and think. But she was rushing forward and they were nearly there. The shape was struggling to sit up. Heavens!

'What the . . .?'

'Dad!' He was just as surprised to see her. Kept rubbing his eyes as if he couldn't believe what he saw. He was rubbing the back of his head too. 'Some blighter banged me one, back of the head. Knocked me cold. Don't know how long I've been out. What's the time?'

Ollie looked at his watch. 'Half past one.'

'Does it hurt anywhere else, Mr Hindmarch? Your leg looks funny.' It did; it was sticking out at a peculiar angle. Hazel had recently been on a first-aid course and was examining it. She seemed to have forgotten the bogle. Had forgotten the 'blighters' who'd knocked Ollie's dad on the head too. Ollie listened and watched.

'Your dad's broken his leg, I think. We must get help. Here Mr Hindmarch' – she was taking off her jacket – 'you must keep warm.'

'No, no, I'm all right. Don't worry about me. It's them blighters we must worry about.' He jerked his head in the direction of the stone circle. 'And Miss Burridge. I came down for her thermos. That's when I was hit. Best if you two get the police I think.'

Ollie's thoughts were racing. Police yes, but later. And yes, they must get her father to hospital, but surely first they must save the bogle. She had a hunch that Burridge was all right.

'Are you two going to stand there all night? At this rate eggs'll be half-way to Saudi Arabia by morning and Cynthia could be at the bottom of crag. Get moving, will you.'

'OK Dad, I'm off, but er . . . first I'll check that Miss Burridge isn't injured higher up. Hazel can stay here with you.'

'No no. Stick together. It's safer. I'm OK.'

'I think he'll be all right for a few minutes, Ollie.'

Despite his protests, Hazel covered him with her jacket and they set off.

Burridge could wait. To the tree first. It was ahead of them, a low silhouette like an enormous hedgehog. When they reached it Ollie held the bogle in her cupped hands while Hazel delved into the tree. For several minutes all she could see were Hazel's legs and the bobbing torch-beam. Then she appeared. 'Right, I've got it I think.' She was holding back the branches. 'There's a hollow between two branches, right near the bottom.' Carefully Ollie moved forward, lowered the bogle into the place Hazel had indicated, gently tipped it into the hole. Waited, though really they shouldn't.

Hazel shone the torch. Its dull ray gave them enough light to see but didn't seem to trouble the bogle who lay still, too, too still. Dry die. Deadwood dreadwood. No! No! Live, bogle, live. *Live*. Crouched on the wet grass, willing it to life, Ollie waited. Waited. Did its knobbly nose quiver? Or did the torch beam waver? She looked at Hazel. Her hand was steady. She looked again. It did move. It did move. The bogle did move. First its nostrils flared, then a claw flexed, and then it was crawling slowly, oh so slowly towards the dark centre of the tree.

'Goodbye, bogle.'

'Good luck.'

They waited until they could see it no more and then stood up and ran. Ran as swiftly and silently as they could, alongside the wall to the stile. And over the stile.

Chapter 17

Burridge, where was she?

The stones stood before them, sparkling in the moonlight, their long shadows stretching towards them. The camouflaged watch-tent was somewhere to their right. More cautious now, they made their way forward. There was the tent, behind a rock. Flapping. Empty. Forward again, listening. Listening. But all they could hear was wind, and water rushing down the rocks. No. Something else. They stopped. Listened. It stopped. There it was again. Kek! Kek! A harsh bird cry pierced the air. Kek! Ke – ek!

They stepped inside the circle. Ollie recognized the cry immediately and her eyes shot to the boulder opposite, the one nearest the edge of the plateau. She ran to the centre of the circle. Saw a rope round the boulder. She dropped to the ground. On their stomachs now, the two of them wriggled forward and then stopped within a metre of the boulder. The red rope was taut from the stone to the plateau edge. As they watched, it vibrated, then moved slightly to one side.

Someone was below. If the peregrines' distress call didn't tell them, the trembling rope did. And Ollie knew who. Like an Indian she moved towards the edge and looked down. Screaming peregrines swooped. Burridge, for despite the black safety helmet, Ollie was sure it was she, hung from the red thread like a fat spider. What now? How could they stop her? What could they do? Ollie thought frantically, wished she knew more about abseiling. Wished for some way to tie the rope to leave Burridge hanging there while she went for help. Caught in the act! Hazel said it was impossible but Ollie still wished. Pictured her dangling there for all to see. How she wished.

And, sensing this, something stirred in the eldertree behind her, something signalled. Something weak growing stronger by the second uttered a high cry inaudible to human ears, which travelled down the fell, over the lake to the island in the middle of Sleadle Water, and the leaves of an eldertree rippled as a creature within it stirred. Over the fell top the cry soared, and down to Bottermere village, to the eldertree by the postbox in the High Street. Up again and over Knotta's Pass to the spindly elder at Brickle Cross and beyond . . . There was a whizzing in the air.

Kek! Kek! Kek! The alarm cries grew more desperate. Was Burridge robbing the nest this instant? They had to do something. Quickly. Quickly. *WHAT*?

'The police?'

'She'll be gone before they come.'

'I wish . . .'

'Listen . . .'

There was a stillness in the air. The wind had dropped. It was lighter too. Dawn streaked the sky purple and blue. And from below came a faint cry of 'Help!'

The girls peered down, following the red rope to the black-suited figure, and then saw why she was in distress. Saw, but could hardly believe their eyes. For the red rope no longer reached the bottom of the crag. The free end was curving upwards, was beginning to coil towards the summit like a charmed snake. Up up it came, looping towards Burridge and she was motionless, paralysed with fear. Ollie felt the hair on the back of her neck prickle. She looked at Hazel. Had she seen it too? She had, so it must be true. Incredible but true. The rope was snaking towards them, slowing now. Stop. Now it started again, this time twisting sideways towards a jutting piece of rock about ten metres from Burridge. Its movements were more complicated now, less regular. The free end rose then fell, rose again, now behind the rock, now in front of it, round again and then a jerk. The rope hung from the rock to which it had tied itself, out of Burridge's reach, making it impossible for her to descend.

But why had she cried for help? Whom did she expect to hear her?

'Look!'

At the bottom of the crag a matchstick figure was galloping towards the car park.

'What shall we do?'

'I don't know. He could be scarpering or he could be coming up to help.'

'Could she climb up again?'

'Yes, but it will take some time.'

'How long?'

'I dunno exactly, Ollie, perhaps half an hour.'

'The police then. And the Mountain Rescue for Dad.'

They raced down the track. Afterwards Ollie couldn't remember climbing the stile. They didn't see the other man but that wasn't surprising. He had an uphill climb, they a downhill run. They were more likely to see him on the next stretch, if he was coming up to help Burridge. Going downhill was harder than expected. Knees felt wobbly and both of them kept slipping.

They reached her dad. He was moaning but stopped when he saw them. He was very pale. Looked worse.

'You'd better go on, Ollie, I'll stay with your dad.'

Ollie took off her jacket, covered him. Hazel whispered, 'Fast as you can, Ol, he looks bad.'

Ollie nearly flew. She didn't meet the man, and when she reached the car park saw the reason why. His car had gone. He'd left Burridge to fend for herself. Ollie found the bikes, pulled one from its hiding place, mounted and pedalled furiously. Where was the nearest phonebox? Her dad needed a doctor desperately. She thought there was one on the road to Helmswick. Hoped so. It would take her at least half an hour to reach the town. If a car passed she'd hitch a lift. No cars but a red blob ahead. She tried to go even faster, reached the box, let the bike drop, could hardly pull the door open. Gasp. Gasp. Dial 999. How on earth would she speak? Someone was speaking. A calm voice.

'Fire, Police or Ambulance. Which service do you require?'

'Er, gasp, ambulance please, I mean Mountain Rescue er . . . and the police please.'

More questions in a clear kind voice, and Ollie managed to tell them where her father was and what had happened on the mountainside.

'Right, lass, stay where you are. We'll pick you up on the way.'

Five minutes later a police car drew up with a policeman and a policewoman inside.

Already there was a helicopter above. By the time they reached her father it was all action. The helicopter was hovering in the nearly-light sky, a rope dangling from its hold. First one man then another descended. A doctor bound her dad's leg and gave him an injection, said he was very brave. Another man strapped him to a stretcher. Then the helicopter came even lower, great gusts of air blasting everything in sight, and Mr Hind-march looking very pale, was swung into the air, hauled into the hold. The door was closed and he was gone.

Ollie looked round. Hazel was standing by her but the two police officers had disappeared.

'They must have gone to get Burridge. Come on, we can't miss this.'

They raced up the track, over the stile for the third time, and into the field.

'Look. There they are.'

The policeman and the policewoman each stood behind a boulder, their backs to the girls, their attention focused on the red rope attached to the stone between them. And as the girls watched they saw first one hand then another grasp the edge of the crag. Just in time they ducked behind a rock as a black safety helmet appeared, then a white face wearing purple-rimmed glasses.

'She must know it's all up, couldn't have missed the helicopter either, and if that didn't scare her the rope trick did.'

Hazel nodded. 'It sure scared me.'

Certainly Burridge looked almost relieved as the police stepped out to arrest her. When Ollie and Hazel darted forward her expression changed to one of fury.

Ollie glared at her. 'The eggs, where are they? And what about my dad?'

She made a feeble attempt to bluff. What did they mean? Where was her father? She was merely checking. Of course she wasn't stealing. The eggs were perfectly all right, in the nest.

'Only because you couldn't get at them,' the police-man intervened, 'and as soon as we get to the station, we shall be charging you with contravention of the Wildlife and Countryside Act, Section 1, Part 1, Clause

8. And then of course there's a little matter of Grievous Bodily Harm and your accomplice. Now are you coming quietly or must we use the cuffs?'

She went quietly and Ollie and Hazel went too. There were statements to make, parents to inform, and of course her dad to visit in hospital. The bogle was safe; the eggs were safe; if her dad were safe then the night would have been very successful.

Chapter 18

It was a Sunday afternoon in July. They came to a bumpy halt in the car park below Ghyll Crag.

'Kangaroo petrol, Rose?'

'Be quiet, Albert, or I won't bring you again.' Mrs Hindmarch got out of the driver's seat and walked round to the passenger side.

'You won't need to, this plaster'll be off next week. Now where're those binoculars.'

'Here Dad.' Ollie and Hazel climbed out of the back.

'Plaster or no plaster, Albert, I've started driving now and I won't stop till I've passed my test.'

'Oh, and then you'll stop, will you?'

'Don't be silly, love.'

Mrs Hindmarch was very proud of her L-plates and very determined to succeed. Mr Hindmarch linked his arm in hers and Ollie was pleased to see him grin.

'Now, do you think you can make it up that slope?'

'Course I can, some of the way, anyhow. Now stop fussing.' They started to walk through the woods still chuntering, but arm in arm.

Ollie and Hazel ran on ahead. They were out of the woods, on the bracken-covered fell, when her dad gave a shout. They turned round. He had the binoculars to his eyes. They looked up, saw grey specks in the sky, ran down again. Ollie took the offered glasses.

'Flying free, as birds should be. Thanks to you, lass – and to you Hazel . . .'

Ollie focused on the shapes in the sky. Thanks, from her dad; that was progress. She saw grey wings flapping furiously. Higher, higher they flew, gliding now, flapping again. Glide. Flap. Glide. She passed the glasses to Hazel.

'Where? Oh yes I see . . . Is this their maiden flight, Mr H?'

'Could be, could be, can't be sure of course, but this is the first time we've seen them. Marvellous.'

It was. They watched in silence. The whole thing was marvellous.

Hazel lowered the glasses. 'They've gone now, over the top. That was fantastic. Gee, I'm sorry Mrs H. We never let you have a look.'

'That's all right, Hazel love. Ollie's dad and me, we'll sit here for a bit now. They may well come back. You and Ollie go and please yourselves for half an hour.'

They strode off up the track, knowing exactly what they would do.

The tree was green and patched with sprays of creamy blossom. From the stile they watched it, saw the blossom sparkle in the sunlight. Closer, a scent like lemonade drifted towards them. They stood, then sat on the grass before the tree. Waited.

Hazel wanted to investigate, pull back the branches, delve into the depths. Ollie wouldn't let her. A skylark trilled on its upward flight and a buzzing bee crawled into a foxglove flower by the wall, but there were no birds in the tree. This was the bogle's tree. It would come if it wanted to and not when called. Elder white love bright. All was well. The bogle knew they were there. Hidden by leaves it listened, watched, wiffled its knobbly nose and sniffed. Turned its head to inspect glossy new scales. If it wanted they would meet again. All was well.